# A

# BROOK

# RUNS

# THROUGH IT

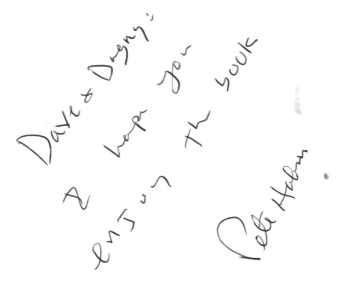

Dave & Dagny:
I hope you
enjoy the book

Pete Helms

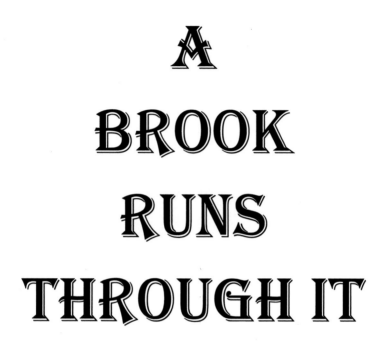

# A BROOK RUNS THROUGH IT

**PETER HUBIN**

*Published by Up North Storytellers*

# A BROOK RUNS THROUGH IT

## PETER HUBIN

Published by: Up North Storytellers
N4880 Wind Rd., Spooner, WI 54801

Library of Congress Control No. 2012935187

ISBN NO. 978-0-615-61572-1

Printed in the United States of America
By: ECPrinting, 415 Galloway St., Eau Claire, WI 54703

This is a coming of age story about Nick, a 14 year old boy who retreats into the wilderness during the summer of 1948. He meets Savannah, a tall, 14 year old redheaded, trout fisherman and they develop a wonderful friendship. The book is fiction but much of it is as things were during that time period in northern Wisconsin.

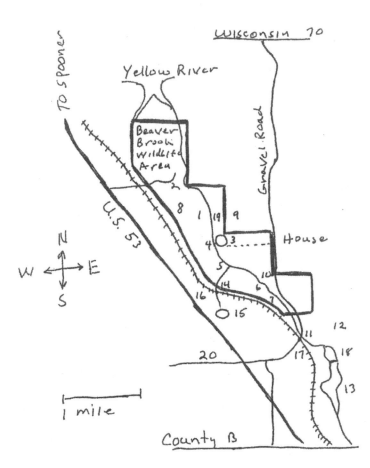

1. Meadows
2. Sandbanks
3. Beaver Pond
4. North Meadow Hole
   Under Cut Hole
   Meadow Curve Hole
   Sluice Dam
5. Camp
6. Upstream Sluice Hole
   Big Sweep Hole
   Straight Hole
7. Northeast Curve Hole
   Steep Bank Hole
   Pine Tree Hole

8. Joe Pachoe Winter Home
9. Old Logging Camp
10. Old Hunters Camp
11. Bridge over Beaver Brook
12. Three Spring Holes
13. Reservoir
14. Railroad Trestle
15. Swamp and Pasture
16. Hilltop Farm
17. Little Dove & Walking
    Bear's home
18. Cranberry Marsh
19. Trappers Cabin
20. Jerry's House

# PREFACE

Nick is a fourteen year old boy who is very interested in the wilderness and feels a great urge to camp out during the summer of 1948. He lives in Spooner, Wisconsin and located just southeast of town is the Beaver Brook Wildlife Area. Nick and his father have hunted in that wildlife area and he has a particular place in mind to set up his camp. There is a grove of large white pines growing on the bank of this beautiful stream called Beaver Brook. He needs to convince his mom and dad to let him camp there for the summer. Nick is one of the top students in his class and he has also learned many things from his mother and father.

His parents give him their approval. His dad helps get a tent and other necessary items and helps Nick plan setting up his camp. His mom helps by being a good worrier and giving Nick a few lessons in food preparation and preservation. Finally, the camp is set up and Nick is on his own.

Very early in the summer, Nick meets Savannah, a tall, red-haired, fourteen-year old girl who is a great trout fisherman. Also entering the picture is Earl, a World War II veteran, severely injured during the battle of Iwo Jima. Earl's war experiences present serious challenges to Nicks summer. Issues arise that may be more than young Nick and Earl can resolve. Nick interacts with both Savannah and Earl throughout the summer. Nick, Savannah and Earl all give to each other but also take something from the others.

Nick meets other people and exploration of this huge forest produces some very interesting discoveries as well as new friendships. Nick and Savannah prove to be excellent trout fishermen and several large trout are caught and released. The beauty of the forest, the constantly flowing streams and the many different animals encountered presents a wonderful natural environment. The ease of Nick's compatibility with all of this makes an interesting story.

This is a coming of age type story and it is fiction. The emotions felt by Savannah and Nick in this deep woods adventure, woven in with other peoples activities makes an easily read story that takes the reader into this forest and stream wonderland as it was in 1948.

# A BROOK RUNS THROUGH IT

**May 11, 1948 - Spring**

My name is Nick, I am 14 years old this spring and I have decided to keep this diary as I am planning an exciting adventure this summer. In the past two years I have read stories about the mountain men like Jim Bridger and others. I have also read stories by Ernest Thompson Seton and the animals he wrote about. I have decided I would like to retreat into the wilderness this summer. I will be all by myself and will rely on my own skills to exist, with a little help from my mom and dad.

I have a place all picked out. I live on High Street in Spooner, Wisconsin. I live with my mother and father and I don't have any brothers or sisters. My dad is an engineer on the railroad and has been driving large trains full of iron ore. There are three diesels on the front and two more pushing on the back until they get over the hump at Sarona.

Last deer season, I went hunting with my dad in the Beaver Brook Wildlife Area southeast of Spooner. The Beaver Brook stream flows the length of this state owned preserve. One day, during the deer season, we came to a beautiful spot near a bend on the stream. There were several large white pines growing close together and the stream was about 50 feet away.

The trees were on a small hill above the stream. The place immediately impressed me as a wonderful place for a campsite, in among these beautiful white pines. For the next several months I thought of what I would need to camp out at that location for the summer of 1948.

The more I thought about it, the more excited I became. I also realized that a project of that size would take much preparation as well as obtaining what ever was needed. I also have to keep everything a secret as I do not want anyone coming to visit me while on this retreat. This will be hard to keep from my friends, Jim and Jed.

I also need to keep it from Mom and Dad until I have things pretty well planned. I am confident Dad will accept me doing this as he is very much an outdoor guy. He loves to hunt and fish, especially trout. Mom, on the other hand, will be a much harder sell. She will worry about me and will be able to imagine all sorts of bad things that could happen. I am sure that when I finally approach both Mom and Dad, I will need Dad's assistance in winning Mom over. Maybe I won't win Dad over, either. Only time will tell and that time is nearly here as school lets out on June 2nd. I hope to be setting up camp on June 3rd.

One part of my plan includes Dad and the railroad, which would run about one quarter of a mile from my proposed campsite. Dad's ore trains run very slow, about four or five miles per hour. My plan, at this time, is to be able to rig up a bag on a stick that I can hold up so my dad could grab it. I could list anything that I need and he could put it in a bag and I can get it as he tosses it to me on a later trip. His train leaves Spooner at 4:17 p.m. on Monday and Friday. At this point, I don't know if Dad will be able to do that. I am hopeful. If it is possible, it may be easier to sell to Mom if she is able to have some contact with me through Dad.

What will I need? For sure, a suitable tent and a tarp to string up to provide a sheltered area for the campsite. The tarp will be tied to the pine trees. Lots of rope will be needed to secure the tarp, but also to keep food in an enclosed pail suspended from a tree branch to discourage hungry animals. I will need a shovel and various pots and pans to do some cooking. Mom could help me there. I am sure I will have to boil my drinking water, so I will need some kind of grate and a safe fire pit. I plan to catch trout and eat them nearly everyday, or every other day. I have a beautiful 8 foot split bamboo fly rod my grandpa Joe gave me. I also have a nice bamboo creel to put the trout in after being caught.

I will need several blankets for inside of the tent. I plan to use pine boughs to sleep on, but a cot may be better. I also plan to keep myself clean so will wash up daily. Clothes will get dirty or wet and it depends on Moms reaction, but I would like to send dirty clothes home with Dad on the train and he could return them next trip. Hopefully Mom will also include cookies, apples, hard boiled eggs and other food that can keep for a few days. She will want to be sure I drink milk and, hopefully, she may have a container that can stand some rough handling.

I will need bug spray and an insect net I can put over my

head. I need to look into getting enough insect netting to make a sitting area under the tarp. I intend to write in this diary nearly every day and, also, one other goal I have for the summer of 1948, is to write a book. I haven't nailed down what it will be yet, but I have several ideas. I will just have to wait and see.

Other things I will need is an axe, plenty of matches, salt, pepper, cornmeal, some lard, toothpicks, toilet paper, tooth brush and toothpaste, aspirins, hip boots, plenty of socks, extra pants and shirts, underwear, jacket, rain coat, handkerchiefs, fishing tackle, hooks, leaders, and bait box. I will make a check list for all items needed.

My plan is to ask Dad to help carry some of the camping materials and help set up the tent and tarp the weekend before school lets out. Hopefully it will fit into his plans. We will have to carry things about one and one-half miles. I also plan to take my .22 rifle and shells with me, in case some animal causes trouble.

I have gone on several trout fishing trips with my dad, but none on the part of Beaver Brook that I plan to fish. We fished further downstream where the stream is bigger and is called the 'sand banks'. I feel confident that my trout fishing skills will be good enough to keep me supplied with trout meals.

One problem ahead of me is what do I tell my friends Jim & Jed? I am leaning toward telling them that I am going to spend the summer with my uncle at his ranch in Montana. I need to tell Mom and Dad about my great summer adventure soon so we can agree on a plan of what we will tell Jim & Jeb and others, if they approve of it. I am pretty sure I can go into the wilderness for the summer, but - there is an occasional doubt that creeps in.

**May 14, 1948.**

I am working on my strategy to tell Mom and Dad about my summer odyssey. Mom is a wonderful lady and she really loves me and supports me in what I have done - up until now. She volunteers at the Methodist Church and belongs to the garden club. She helps serve lunch for funerals at the Methodist Church. She also makes quilts, which she sells. Mom is 35 years old and is attractive. She seems to be a typical mother/housewife of our time. She wears house dresses nearly every day and I think she is quite talented and is a very nice person. I am sure she loves me and I love her.

Dad is a quiet, soft spoken man that is good at his job which is being a train engineer. Both Mom and Dad grew up in Spooner and both graduated from Spooner High School back in the 1930s. Dad is a careful worker and is well respected by his fellow workers. He really loves to hunt and fish which he does whenever he can. He is a very friendly person, who can visit with anyone. He and Mom both read *The Superior Evening Telegram* and several magazines. Both seem well informed about what goes on in the world but they don't seem to gossip. I have decided to state my case on May 17th, after supper. I have also added the following to my check list of things to take: a hunting knife, pocket knife, needle nose pliers, this book and another one like it, several pens and pencils, band-aids, rubbing alcohol, bars of soap, extra pair of shoes, extra cap, two pair of work gloves, small Swede saw and flashlight and batteries.

## May 17, 1948 - Late afternoon.

Well, I broke the news to Mom and Dad after supper. I guess I dropped a bomb on them. It was all quite embarrassing. I told them what I wanted to do and it was all quiet - for a long time! Finally, they began asking questions. Wasn't I happy at home? Won't you be scared? Why do you want to do something like this? Isn't it dangerous? We discussed a few things and finally Dad said they needed to think it over. We could talk again tomorrow night. I agreed and asked them not to say anything to anybody. They agreed.

## May 18, 1948 - Late.

Mom and Dad had talked it over and were very concerned about several things. Mom was a real worry wart and she was sure bad people lurked in the woods and could harm me. She worried about if I got sick or hurt. Dad wondered if extreme wind, rainfall, insects and other things like animals could be a threat to my safety. In the end of our discussion, they both reluctantly agreed to let me proceed.

Dad was pretty sure he could drop off things from his train and also pick up a small bag on the return trip. Dad had inquired about camping on the states wildlife area and it was an approved activity. I did not press the issue wondering if it had to be in an approved area. It was good enough for me.

We talked about the need to keep this project quiet. I told them what I planned to tell my friends, Jim and Jed. They agreed and came up with a logical story about Mom's brother who actually lived in Montana, but did not have a ranch. He will by the time I get there. Actually, we didn't need to worry about Jim or Jed. Jim was going to spend the summer in Milwaukee with his paternal grandparents. Jed was taking a long trip with his grandmother. They were going to tour the west and then he would help her paint her house in Rochester, Minnesota.

**May 19, 1948**

I showed my list to Mom and Dad and we did some planning. I had saved $119 and hoped that would cover most of what I needed. I really hoped Mom and Dad would chip in with things on the list and some cash to purchase what was needed.

The tent and tarp were good starting items as Dad thought we would need to go to Superior to buy the tent and maybe the tarp. I wanted them to be camouflaged.

The tent would be 5' by 6' with side walls on it. If possible it should have a canvas floor as part of the tent. We decided to go to Superior on Saturday and visit an army surplus store on Belnap Avenue. This store may have other items needed like an entrenching tool which would be a small shovel.

**May 22, 1948**

The army surplus store was a great place to buy items on my list. The tent was just what I wanted. I would be able to stand up in it as I am 5' 9" tall. I may have to duck my head. The price was $21.95. The tarp was 12' by 16' and it was olive  drab color as was the tent. That is good because I want the camp site to be difficult to see by anyone fishing on the stretch of Beaver Brook near the site. I also bought an entrenching tool, 80 feet of ¼ inch rope, ten - tent stakes, three - one gallon plastic jars for water, two - five quart pans for boiling water and other things. I also found a nice grill to put over the campfire. All these items cost another $19, not counting the tent.

Getting all these items home and in the house was exciting. We spent most of the day going to Superior. Dad wanted to go trout fishing on the Clam River and he asked me to go with him. I will go with Dad and I really enjoyed going with him to Superior.

**May 24, 1948**

Wow! Dad and I really caught some nice German Brown trout on Clam River. We went near the Sour Bean Dam and two of our catch weighed over three pounds apiece. I just realized I will need a reliable clock of some kind, also a calendar. I really worked my brain to come up with all the items needed on my exciting, but scary adventure.

I wonder if Tom Sawyer had a list as long as mine. Besides, he had to carry it all on a raft. Oh, well, it worked for Tom, I just hope it will work for me. Dad found a large knapsack which he felt I would need to get my things to the camp after school was out. He will be driving the train and would not be able to help after the weekend. Mom will have to take me to the jump off point in our trusty '37 Ford. I will have to carry my stuff down the tracks to the south for about one and one-quarter miles. Then into the woods for about a quarter of a mile to the camp.

## May 27, 1948

Mom and I have gone through my list several times - each time she adds an item or two. I remind her that Dad and I have to carry all this stuff about one and one-half miles. I really appreciate Mom's participation. I think this has been an adventure for both Mom and Dad, as well as me. The entire thing scares me at times. Jim and Jed stopped over and we decided to fish below the dam on the Yellow River. We dug worms, which reminded me, I need to dig worms and find a place to keep a bunch of them so I can catch enough trout for three or four meals per week. I have already decided that I would not catch more than two limits, or 20 trout per week all summer. Less if it looks like the population can't stand that many, or my trout catching skills are not good enough. I know that I can not catch more than I can eat in two consecutive meals. No refrigeration. In fact, Mom and Dad just got a refrigerator last year in 1947. Long waiting list because of World War II.

## May 28, 1948

The three of us caught several fish below the dam. Jim and Jed were both somewhat concerned about their summer adventures. Both seemed worried about what they did not know about. I continued getting things on my list. Some I had to buy, or ask Mom and Dad to buy, so it didn't cause anyone to get an idea of what was about to happen.

## May 31, 1948 - Sunday.

Dad and I will carry the tent, tarp and lots of large items

into the campsite. The plan is for Mom to drive us to the railroad crossing on the way to the sand banks. Dad and I will get out and head south down the tracks. Mom will come back at 4:00 p.m. to pick us up.

**May 31, 1948 - Late.**

We carried things to the campsite and studied the area to decide the best location for the tent and tarp. Also under consideration was location of a fire pit and a slit trench for bathroom use. We finally decided on the location of all these components. We hung up the tarp between five large white pines. Next, we located the tent under the tarp but toward the south edge. We put a shallow trench around the tent and built up the area under the tent with pine needles. At the last minute, I decided sleeping on a cot was better than pine boughs, so I had bought one at the hardware store.

I planned to build a fire only in the evening. Cooking a hot meal once every other day was what I was planning to do. I would use these fires to boil water to make it safe to drink. We located the grill over the fire pit. We searched and finally found enough rocks to line the fire pit. We also dug the litter away down to bare dirt to prevent a spark from starting a fire. Dad told me about birch bark being able to light on fire even if it is wet. I could see several white birch trees fairly close by. Dad told me that the lower dead limbs on the white pine should be added to the fire next. Once this small fire is going good, larger pieces of wood could be added.

We took the saw and axe and looked for dead trees that we could cut into 16 or 20 inch lengths. Larger pieces needed splitting, which we did. By the time we left, we had a decent pile of wood under the tarp. I can see that rounding up wood will take a fair amount of time. If I was smart, I would range out further and not use all the dead wood near by.

We put the food pail suspended up over a strong limb. I had painted it brown and green to make it more difficult to see. The rope we used was olive drab in color. Finally we packed up and hiked back so we could get picked up by Mom at 4:00 p.m.

The tent will be my home all summer. It seemed like a cozy, secure abode. I could just stand up in it and it had a three foot side wall. I will sleep on the west side and use the east side to store various things, but not food.

**June 1, 1948 - Late.**

Last full day of school today. One-half day tomorrow. I spent all evening getting the last of what I need at camp. I realized that there is more than I can carry by myself. I decide what is most important and pack that in the knapsack. Mom dug out a duffel bag and a small suitcase. She helped and we packed both of these. I hoisted the knapsack on my back and picked up the duffel bag and suitcase. That was a big load. Mom suggested I leave some of the canned food to be delivered by Dad and the train. We repacked and now I felt I could carry this load tomorrow. Mom will drop me off at the same place Dad and I started from. This will be after I get home from the half-day of school.

I hope Jim and Jed don't want to come over or have me

go to their house.  I decide that I will have a bad headache and must go home and lie down.

We load the knapsack, duffel bag and suitcase in the trunk of the '37 Ford and it is in the garage.  I will lie down on the floor of the back seat.  Mom is pretty nervous about all of this but she thinks it will work.

## June 2, 1948 - Late.

WOW!  I am at my camp.  Boy, it was a struggle lugging all my stuff from the car to camp.  Knapsack on my back, duffel bag and suitcase in each hand along with fish pole and .22 rifle.  No fire tonight, so ate a can of Spam.  Feel quite comfortable in my tent.  Nearly dark.  Goodnight.

## June 3, 1948 - Early.

Poor nights sleep.    There was a lot of animal noise around.  Heard something sniffing outside the tent.  Scary. Tree frogs and others sang most of the night.  Heard two owls hooting fairly close.  As I was eating Cheerios with condensed milk for breakfast, a half grown red fox came right up to within a few feet away.  It was very curious.  I tossed a couple Cheerios toward it.  Surprise - the fox ate them.  In a few minutes, two other half grown foxes came running up.  All three stayed around for about an hour and then ran off toward the southeast.  I went exploring up stream.    Put hip boots on and crossed the stream.    I walked into several holes to find out where trout might be for future catching.  Went to the big pine tree on a corner. This tree is a white pine and must be over four feet in diameter.  It is the largest tree I have ever seen.  This hole is about as good looking trout hole as I have ever seen.  I waded into it and saw a very large fish leave. It was at least three pounds and very likely was a trout. I explored the hole with my foot. Lots of pine roots but ideal for trout.

In late afternoon, I dug some worms out of my stash in a buried bucket and slipped into the stream above a nice looking long run hole. I let the worm float into the edge of the main run. I caught two nice fat 8 ½ inch brook trout. I moved toward the far end of this long hole. No luck, but - - as I fished, all of a sudden a large trout jumped out and caught a butterfly that was flying over the water. This fish really scared me and I am guessing it weighed three pounds. That is probably why I didn't catch anything in that part of the hole. This big bruiser probably eats any smaller trout. I made a fire to cook trout, but also to boil water to make it safe to drink. I rolled the trout in corn meal, put lard in frying pan and put two quarts of water in a pan to boil. Trout tasted really great. I made a peanut butter sandwich and ate an apple. I carried the trout bones down away from camp and buried them. I went to the stream and scrubbed the pan in stream water and soap. The water boiled. I have a four gallon shotgun can with a cover to keep the water in. I used one of Mom's funnels with layers of cheese cloth to filter the water. The shot gun can is tied to two stakes driven in the ground to keep it from getting tipped over. I hope to get more sleep tonight. This was an outstanding day, about 75° F. with clear sky. My first day in camp was very exciting.

### June 4, 1948 - Early.

There was more noise outside the tent last night. I heard

sniffing and sounds like something walking. About midnight, I heard a terrible scream! It scared me big time. I grabbed the .22 rifle. It sounded about 100 feet away. I ventured out of the tent with the flashlight and gun. I did not see anything. I finally realized it may have been a wildcat or bobcat.

I heard owls and tree frogs. I heard very high pitched song coming from the stream. I wonder what it is. Could be a frog or toad. I also heard a loud splash in the stream. Not much sleep again last night.

I had Cheerios with condensed milk and an orange for breakfast. Mom insisted I get milk and orange juice. She bought a bunch of those small cans of evaporated milk. While we were planning this adventure, Mom and Dad insisted that all cans, bottles and boxes would get sent home with Dad. I washed the can out and put it in a sack to give to Dad. The orange peelings went into the slit trench and are covered from time to time. I made a peanut butter sandwich and wrapped it in waxed paper and put it in my shoulder pouch along with the last of the hard boiled eggs Mom sent. I am headed for that big pine tree hole to see if I can tell where that big trout hangs out.

**June 4, 1948 - Late.**

It is a beautiful day. Boy, did I get a surprise! I crawled in beside the giant pine tree and had been watching the activity in the hole for about an hour. I saw the three pounder and also a large trout of about two pounds. I could see where it was hanging out by a large root. I looked up and here comes a fisherman, or fisher girl. She was approaching the hole from upstream and was in the stream wearing hip boots. She had red hair! It was in a pony tail coming out of the back of her cap. She was very well equipped with vest, creel and net. She began fishing the hole and had not seen me. I quietly said, "There is a two pounder right below my hand." I pointed down. I did really scare her as she was very intent on fishing. I suggested she retrieve her line and put her bait in another part of the rapids. She pulled her line and I noticed she was using a wet fly for bait. She maneuvered the fly in the current and it went right to the two pounder and it grabbed the fly. Right now this girl set the hook and began playing this fish. Twice it jumped out of the water, but the girl kept it from getting tangled into the roots of the giant tree.

The battle went on for 7-8 minutes and then the girl reached for her net and skillfully brought the exhausted fish into the net. That girl was quite the fisherman. After she caught the big trout, I got up from my spot by the tree and joined her at midstream  as I congratulated her on doing a great job catching this beauty. She said, "Thanks, but I have to measure it and put it back." She took out a tape measure and found the German Brown trout was 17-½ inches long. She then proceeded to remove the wet fly from its mouth and waded into deeper water and gently released it back into the depths.

I could see she was about my age, around 5'6" or 5'7" tall and of medium build. She was good looking!!! I asked her what her name was and she replied it was Savannah. I told her my name.  Her parents have a cabin by Birchwood, Wisconsin and they come there every summer. They live at Antigo, Wisconsin where her dad is a teacher and her mom is a nurse. She will be a freshman in the fall.

Their school just got out and this was the first time fishing Beaver Brook this summer. I told her I went to school at Spooner and it also just got out for the summer and I will also be a freshman this fall. I didn't tell her about my camp. I offered to share my peanut butter sandwich and hard boiled eggs. To my surprise, she accepted my offer and we sat on the edge of the stream with our feet in the water and we shared lunch.

Savannah said her mom and dad were fishing behind her and should show up soon and I could meet them. I asked her why she released the big trout. She said, "We fish because we enjoy the challenge and we really like the solitude of a trout stream. We will keep enough for each of us to eat one meal each time we fish."

She wanted to know where my fly rod was. I told her I was just scouting the stream and will fish later. I did tell her about the larger trout still in this beautiful hole. I intend to scout it and when the conditions are favorable I will try to catch it.

I noticed three strange looking lures hanging on her vest. I asked her and she said, "They are Mepps French Spinners. They are made in Antigo by a fellow by the name of Sheldon. He was in France during World War II and saw fisherman catching trout with them. He worked out a deal for exclusive rights to make and sell these spinners in America. I think some parts come from France. I don't use this rod with the spinner. I have a spinning rod and it really works on bigger water. Maybe I can show you my spinning rod and we can fish some bigger water." I told her about the beaver pond about three-quarters of a mile away. I told her that I can't reach out far enough with my fly rod.

About this time, two fisherman appeared upstream and Savannah said, "There are my mom and dad." When they reached us, Savannah introduced me to them. They were Elon and Kathy Casey and they are very nice. Savannah told of catching the 17 ½ inch brown trout and releasing it. She told them, "Nick had scouted the hole and was lying by the big tree and told me where to put the fly and it worked." She told about sharing my lunch with her. Nick is scouting today and told me that there is a three pounder, or larger, in those tree roots. I was getting nervous and wanted to leave, but I also wanted to see Savannah again. "Any idea when you might be back to try those spinners on the beaver pond?" Her dad and mom conferred and finally said, "How about next Tuesday?" I said, "What time? Right here by the big pine?" Elon said, "How about 9:00 a.m.?"

I said goodbye and would meet Savannah next Tuesday at 9:00 a.m. Boy what a surprise to meet such a nice girl and she is a great fisherman. I really like her.

No fire tonight. Had peanut butter sandwiches and an apple. The three foxes showed up as I was eating. All three came about three feet away from me. Boy, they are quick inquisitive rascals. I tossed a small bit of a sandwich and all smelled of it and finally one grabbed it and ate it. One fox nearly smelled my outstretched finger but could not quite do it.

I am lying in my tent writing. I hear a kingfisher near the

stream. Crows are calling in the distance. I think some of the crow noise is by baby crows that have left the nest.

I have many ideas for a book rolling around in my mind. I really want to write a story by the end of the summer. Meeting Savannah today has distracted my thinking. It's my third night and I hope I can get a good nights sleep. It was another beautiful June day. Even though the mosquitoes were not out today, I think I got bit at the big pine tree hole today, by a beautiful, tall, red-haired girl.

## June 5, 1948 - Early.

I had a better nights sleep. I heard snorting about midnight. It woke me up and I grabbed the gun and went out with the flashlight. I saw a huge buck with his antlers in the velvet. He snorted a few times and then walked off toward the south. I heard owls, tree frogs and other frogs or toads. While looking at the buck, I saw three or four fire flies. What an interesting insect.

I had Cheerios, milk and an orange for breakfast. Mom mixed up a batch of soda and salt for me to brush my teeth with each morning. My drinking water supply is getting low so I will have to have a fire tonight and that means I need to catch two or three trout later today.

I plan to scout holes to the north today. Several good looking trout holes. The first hole was the 'steep bank' I waded in and felt the bottom. Next was the 'northeast curve' and the 'big sweep'. These are all my names. Next comes the 'straight hole' by the water coming from the beaver pond. Next is the 'upstream sluice' and then the 'sluice hole'. Just down from that is the 'meadow curve'. This spring there has been good rainfall so the 'Beaver' is running full, but not overflowing.

I make a mental note about each hole, especially the shape of the bottom where trout like to lie and wait for food to come down stream to them. I did see three nice trout in the two to three pound class. As I waded down stream, I saw one good sized water snake which scared me big time. A short distance later, I saw a doe and two fawns on a sandbar just above the big sweep hole. They did not see me and I watched for several minutes. The fawns romped while the doe watched, but eventually the two little spotted twerps realized they were hungry and they both started sucking - on the same side at once. Both little tails were just wagging. That was a beautiful sight. Eventually the doe took the fawns and crossed the stream and disappeared to the west. I waited for ten minutes as to not alarm the deer family.

I passed through the straight hole just above the stream

coming from the beaver pond. There was a distinctive drop in temperature in the water from the beaver pond. One problem for the trout in the 'Beaver' is that it flows through a cranberry marsh which has a large reservoir that allows the water to warm up. Brook trout require cold water whereas brown trout can do alright in warmer water. Anyway, that is what my dad told me.

The next hole is the upstream sluice hole. This is a deep hole, deeper than I could wade through. That is a good sign. Next is the sluice hole, probably the most intriguing hole on the 'Beaver'. Apparently, long ago, loggers built a sluice dam here to hold back a huge body of water as snow melted in the spring. Throughout the winter, loggers cut pine logs and piled them along the stream, downstream from the dam. During the previous fall, loggers got rid of any places where logs could jam up.

At the appropriate time, the dam was opened or blown up with dynamite. This released the huge amount of water behind the dam. Loggers rolled the logs into this torrent and were on their way to the appropriate sawmill. Loggers with pike poles are stationed by any potential 'log jam' site.

When this dam was built, it was part of a natural bowl that loggers put four 12" x 12" timbers at least 25 feet long across the stream. These were spaced about four feet apart and were imbedded in the ground on both sides. These timbers are mostly in the water but the tops are out of the water. This causes the water to flow very differently and as I feel the bottom and sides with my feet, I find three beautiful holes. Two holes are on the west side and one between the first and second timbers.

Down stream 150 feet is the meadow curve. This is a long sweep that flows under the bank and my feet tell me that it is an outstanding trout hole. This is the beginning of the terrain called the 'meadows'. For whatever reason, very few trees or brush grow there and it mostly has grown up to grass. Also, by now the 'Beaver' is more than double the size that it was by the big pine hole. Several springs add their water plus the large springs in the beaver pond.

My scouting trip impressed me with the many possible outstanding holes. Not only that, but this stream is beautiful with great scenery. Huge white pines are abundant as are many large elm trees. Steep banks and hills add to the beauty. Where my camp is located requires much walking to get to that part of the stream from any road. I don't expect to see many fishermen near the camp. I return to camp, but on the way I nearly step on a mother ruffed grouse and her brood of about twelve babies. In late afternoon I dig up some fat worms out of my stash. I take my split bamboo eight foot fly rod and my creel and head to the straight hole. I waded into the stream above the hole and stay bent over to avoid being seen by the wary trout. I float the worm and let out line. I found a small log earlier and work the worm along the log - bang! A fat nine and one-half inch brookie smacks the bait. I set the hook and I have it. It runs down stream, but I can hold it and, in about one minute, I tire it enough to lift it out. I admire the beautiful spots. I use my needle nose pliers and remove the number 6 snelled hook. I find some grass to put in my bamboo creel and then put this beauty in the creel.

Amazingly, the worm was OK to use - in fact the worm

was strung on the leader.  I have seen this several times before.  I re-hooked the worm and moved to the west side of the rapids leading into the straight hole.  I float the worm along the bank and as it came near an overhang part of the bank a fat eight inch brookie slipped out and snarfed up the worm.  I set the hook and it went across the current and really put up a fight.  After two trips back and forth, I was able to lift it out and put it on the bank.  I removed the hook and put this beauty in the creel.

My fishing is done for today so I take my rod apart as it joints in the middle.  The rod is easier to 'drive' through underbrush.  I move upstream to an exposed sandbar and use my hunting knife to clean the trout for supper.

I return to camp and start a fire.  I get two sauce pans full of water and put them on the grill above the fire.  Besides the trout, I will eat an apple and a small can of mixed fruit.  I roll the trout in corn meal and remove one pan of water.  I put the skillet on the grill and put the trout in.  The trout are cooked with their heads on as there are some choice bites of meat in the cheeks of the trout.  Some societies eat the eyes, but not me.  It doesn't take long and the trout are cooked.  I put the pan of water back on the grill.  Boy, those trout were good.  I clean the frying pan with grass and take it to the stream and scrub it with sand and dish soap.  I rinse it and return to camp.  I take the fish bones about 100 feet away and use my shovel to bury them and the apple core.  The can the fruit was in is washed and stashed in the bag to go home.

If everyday was as full as this one, I will really have an exciting time.  It is nearly dark and I am ready to turn in.  I still have no idea for a story.  Too much excitement.

Maybe tomorrow. I hope I can get a good nights sleep. I have strung up the mosquito netting in anticipation of their visit.

## June 6, 1948 - Early Saturday.

May see other trout fishermen and fisherwomen today. Slept good last night. Heard crashing once. Heard the owls. It sounds like several of them. Perhaps a family. Nothing came around sniffing, at least I didn't hear it. The kingfisher woke me about dawn. I laid here listening. I identify crows, a robin, a woodpecker pounding on a tree. There are lots of tweety birds which I cannot identify. There was a faraway scream and it sounded scary. I can hear some animals running around and I peek out and there are the three half-grown foxes. I come out of the tent and sit on my camp stool and all three come very close and one just about touches my hand as it sniffs my outstretched hand. They roughhouse with each other and, after about ten minutes, they make their way toward the south and are out of sight in a few minutes.

Today I am going to the beaver pond to size it up so when Savannah comes Tuesday I might have an idea about where to fish, etc. It would really be cool to have some sort of raft, but I don't have any raft making materials.

## June 6, 1948 - Late Saturday.

I went to the beaver pond. Saw fresh cutting where beaver have been logging. I did see two beaver swimming. There is more open water on the east side but the bank is fairly steep so it would be difficult to fish there. The beaver pond is about five acres and has areas of marshy growth as well as several dead trees standing out in the water. I did wade out in several places and using a stick, low and behold, I found a spot that I could wade about 100 feet from shore. At that point the water was getting much deeper according to my hip boots and the stick I was using. It looked like I was on the very edge of a deep spring hole. I carefully made my way back to shore and gathered up four sticks about four feet long. I proceeded out into the pond again and pushed a stick in the bottom, but it was out of the water. By the time I used all four sticks I was back at the edge of deep spring. I watched for trout, but could not see any. I was confident that there were plenty there.

The beaver pond is an unusual water formation. Large hills surround the entire pond except on the west side where this very cold water runs out and into Beaver Brook about 100 feet away. The springs in this pond put out a tremendous stream of water. The beaver dam on the west side was only about 50 to 60 feet long and four to five feet high. It was an impressive structure. The one problem I could see is that the beaver have used up the available trees nearby and the steep banks hinder their labors. A great blue heron flew in and landed near shore on the southwest part of the pond.

I return to camp and check two sand bars to see if anyone fished near camp today. I found tracks of one person. I have peanut butter sandwiches, an apple and an orange. Tomorrow, Mom and Dad will visit my camp in the afternoon. They wanted to visit every other Sunday afternoon and that was fine with me. I hope Mom brings some fried chicken. I can hear a catbird nearby and am fascinated by its great variety of songs.

**June 7, 1948 - Early.**

Cool morning - overcast - maybe rain. Heard something sniffing outside the tent last night. It is a fairly large animal, maybe a raccoon. Later I heard some rustling noise and smelled a skunk. Hope it doesn't come back. I can hear blue jays, crows and tweety birds. I go down to the stream and find strange tracks on a sand bar. They are small, about the size of a small cat. Will ask Dad this afternoon.

**June 7, 1948 - Late.**

Mom and Dad got to camp about 1:30 p.m. Mom did bring fried chicken, which we ate. She also baked an apple pie and brought two pieces for me, plus one each for Mom and Dad. Mom brought four hard boiled eggs, more canned milk, cookies, apples and oranges. Also a small sausage and fresh bread. She put in one Mounds candy bar. Dad looked at the tracks on the sand bar and thought it was a mink. He said they are relatives of the skunk so what I smelled might have been a mink.

Mom seemed nervous when she arrived. By the time we had eaten she seemed to get comfortable in the camp. I think she just needed to see the camp and see me. Apparently she feels I am getting along OK. Mom said my friend Jim had gone to Milwaukee and Jed just left by bus to go to his grandmothers house at Rochester, Minnesota. Jim wondered how you left without them seeing any car around. Mom told him that her brother arrived late one night and you both left early the next morning for Montana.

Mom said that the shoe store just started a contest. Points are awarded for each pair of shoes someone buys. The person can award these points to anyone. Mom was going to go in and buy a pair of shoes and give the points to me! She said the rules called for kids ages 14 and younger to get the points. Nice prizes like a Daisy BB gun, baseball glove, roller skates, dolls and many other prizes. It ends about the time I plan to return home. Mom said the Indians from near Hayward will have their first summer pow-wow this coming Friday evening. They perform at the park by the railroad depot. I really enjoyed watching the young Indian boys and girls perform. Guess I will miss this activity this year. Maybe they will still be dancing and chanting when I get home.

I walked with Mom and Dad up to the railroad tracks. Mom took some dirty clothes and the empty cans back with them. I felt a little sad when I hugged them good-bye. I know I can come home anytime I want but so far I am really enjoying my adventure. I did  tell the folks about Savannah. That girl seems to be on my mind - often.

**June 8, 1948 - Early.**

The owls really hooted last night. Lightning bugs really active last night, too. Heard a deer snort in the night. Also heard the sniffer again. Moon is almost full. I sat outside the tent from 9:30 to 10:30. No mosquitoes at that time of the night. I can hear them in the trees but they don't sting me. About dusk, the little devils really get after me.

## June 8, 1948 - Late.

After breakfast, I took my .22 and went downstream to the old sluice dam. I crossed to the east side of the 'Beaver' and headed up on the hill to the east. I had never been in this part of this huge forest and the combination of the ridges and hardwood trees made for some beautiful scenery. I can see the beaver pond in the distance to the south. I decide to go toward the north. I found the remnants of an old trail! The vehicles made ruts in the ground and fairly large trees have grown up between the ruts. I follow the ruts as they ran northeast. I could see a large hill looming to my right as the tracks seemed to be skirting the hill.

I watched the tracks carefully and I detected a faint set of tracks that went off to the southeast. I decided to try to follow those tracks. I made a small blaze on a blue beech tree so I could find the original trail if I lost my way. I do carry a compass at all times.

These faint tracks seemed to be aimed at the base of this big hill. I followed and they seemed to end at the bottom of the hill. I looked around. I looked up the hill to both sides. I did not see anything out of the ordinary. There was a large oak tree that had been blown down and was near the base of the hill. That event had occurred many years ago. I blazed a small shrub near the end of the trail and headed for the downed tree.

I got near the tree and saw several small saplings growing in the branches of this large tree. It appeared to have a dark spot deep in the branches. There appeared to be something much darker than the surrounding area, under the tree. I found a long stick and picked it up and headed into the downed tree top. I got close enough so I poked the dark area with the stick. There was nothing to poke! There appeared to be a hole under this tree top. I was able to squeeze further into the tree top. Still no end to the hole.

I could not get any closer, but I squinted my eyes and I could make out part of a door jamb - I thought. It would have opened to the west. I backed out of the tree top and began to circle around it to the left. My foot hit against a rusted out pan. I took a stick and rooted around near the rusty pan. I found part of a china plate, several small plate parts turned up also. I continued around the tree top and above the apparent door I found the remnants of a chimney. There must be a room below my feet. Now I was really excited. I also realized that I better get off the roof of this dugout or I might find myself taking a fast trip inside. I continued toward the southwest and found the remnants of a steel chair. It appeared to have a broken leg and was partly covered with dirt. I took a stick and scratched around and found a rusted coffee pot. Who lived here?

Was this home to an old bachelor? A young family? Was this a hideout for one of the infamous 'gang members' of Al Capone's gang, or some other mobster on the run. It was well known that the Chicago Mobster, Al Capone, retreated to this northwest part of Wisconsin and apparently owned property in the area. Wow! That is an exciting thought. Maybe it could have been a logger. He would need horses or oxen to pull logs to a landing somewhere. Maybe he cut them in the winter and piled the logs on the banks of Beaver Brook below the sluice dam. When the dam was opened, the logs were rolled into this huge flowing water. The logs would have made their way down river to the sawmill that owned the logs. My dad told me about these logging camps because his dad, my grandpa, worked in two camps when he was a young man. Both camps had 25 to 35 men working in them and they built their own bunkhouses, cook shanty and other buildings out of logs. I really doubt that this dugout belonged to a logger.

My dad also told me that just about all the land in this county was owned by people or companies like logging companies. The depression of the 1930s was so severe that thousands of people could not pay their taxes or payments on their farms, homes and businesses so huge amounts of land reverted to county ownership and later became county forest land which is open to the public. I don't know how or when the State of Wisconsin got possession of the Beaver Brook Wildlife Area. My guess is that the dugout belonged to a settler and the depression came along and they lost the land because of failure to pay taxes or payments. There could be other reasons. Maybe they died from some disease like scarlet fever. Mom lost one of her brothers to scarlet fever in 1936. Maybe they just moved away. Maybe it was a hunting camp. There are a lot of maybes.

I meet Savannah tomorrow and we will go fishing on the beaver pond. I want to show her the dugout and I will take my flashlight with me. I am sure looking forward to seeing Savannah tomorrow. She sure is pretty.

## June 9, 1948 - Early.

Full moon last night. Clear sky and the moon shining down through the trees, especially the big pines in the campsite, was very pleasing. The owls were at it again. I sat up later than normal after the mosquitoes gave up. Heard rustling near the stream and my flashlight revealed a mink sniffing along the stream. Fireflies were out again. Heard a loon flying over, laughing like crazy. There are lots of critters active at night, large and small. I hear some bird like sounds coming from the leaves nearby that I can't identify. Finally I hear two tree frogs singing back and forth.

## June 9, 1948 - Late.

I met Savannah by the big tree by 9:00 a.m. She had her spinning rod and one for me to use. She seemed quite shy this morning. We headed to the beaver pond and did not fish until we got there. Her folks planned to fish on the stream while we fished the beaver pond.

We got to the pond and went where I had put the sticks in the water to mark the path to the edge of the deep spring hole. Before we stepped into the water, we heard what sounded like someone pumping water with an old hand pump. It was coming from out in the pond where there were rushes and cattails. Neither of us had ever heard that sound before and really wondered what it was.

Savannah handed me the spinning rod with a number two Mepps French spinner on it. She gave a short demonstration and we stepped into the water. We followed the sticks to near the edge of the deep spring hole. Savannah made the first cast. She let the spinner settle a bit and started reeling it in. Wham!! A nice fat brook trout nailed the spinner. Savannah played the fish out and brought it to the net. She measured it and found it to be 13 ¼ inches long and then she released it. I made a cast - nothing. Finally, on my fifth cast, I got a good strong hit. I played it out and Savannah netted it. We measured it and found it to be 12 ½ inches long. I removed the spinner and released this beautiful fish.

Using that spinning rod and spinner was easy and a lot of fun. We fished about one hour and caught seven more trout from 8 ½ inches to a 14 inch brook trout. All were returned to the pond.

While we fished, we visited. Savannah had to return to Antigo for a dentist appointment. She got started with braces on her teeth. She seems to be getting along just fine so far. I told her about the dugout I found and asked if she wanted to see it. She said she really wanted to see it. Maybe it is haunted.

By now it was about noon and I had packed a peanut butter sandwich for each of us. I wrapped them in waxed paper. We found a place to sit and munch. Just then, two beavers swam by. I waved my hand and both beaver slapped the water with their tails and dove out of sight. Man, that slap was loud. It sounded like two large rocks being dropped in the water.

We stashed our fish poles and headed around the east end of the pond. We frightened a great blue heron and it flew toward the west. It didn't take long to get to the dugout. I showed Savannah the pans, china and chair I found yesterday. I shined the flashlight into the dark spot in the tree top. There was just too much vegetation in the way and I could not see much. I definitely could see what I thought was a door jamb yesterday and my flashlight confirmed it.

I tried to crawl in a little further and now I could get my flashlight beam into the opening, but I still could not see much. I invited Savannah to crawl in and take a peek and she did. This big tree was just too large to deal with. I did see one smaller limb that I might be able to cut off with my small saw. With that limb gone maybe we could crawl in far enough to see into the dugout.

We backed out and brushed ourselves off. Savannah wanted to look for more pots and things so we took sticks and rooted around. We found some rusty cans and two bottles that were blue. Savannah was really curious about the dugout. She really wanted to find out who lived there. The next time I will take the saw and see if I can cut the limb off. By now it was time to head back to the beaver pond and pick up our gear. I needed to start a fire and sterilize drinking water so I suggested that we wade out and try to catch enough trout for my supper. Savannah's first cast produced a fat 12 ½ inch brook trout. She measured and recorded it in her journal and then gave it to me. "Happy supper," she said. We made our way to the big pine tree and her mom and dad were just getting there also. They had caught many trout including a 17 inch brown trout that they released. They showed us their creels and they only kept five trout between them and they appeared to be in the nine to eleven inch range. Her dad said he caught a horned dace, also known as a stoneroller. These are undesirable fish so it was not released.

Savannah's parents were very interested in my campsite. I offered to meet them there the next time they fished the 'Beaver'. Savannah told them about the dugout and wanted to come back as soon as they could. They thought they could be back on Thursday and they would meet me at my campsite. I told them I would keep watching for them as they fished downstream. I thanked Savannah for letting me use the spinning rod. We said goodbye and Savannah touched my hand as she left - WOW!!! That felt great. She really is a very nice girl and she sure has pretty red hair.

I get a fire going in the fire pit and put two pots of water on to boil. I fry the trout and eat two slices of Mom's bread plus an apple. I bury the bones and the apple core some distance from camp. Boy, today was exciting.

## June 10, 1948 - Late.

By mid-afternoon the rain stopped. I took my fly rod and worms and went to the big pine tree hole. The 'Beaver' was higher as we must have gotten two to three inches of rain. I approached the hole from upstream and with one split shot on my line, I floated a worm right into the roots of this giant tree. I felt a fish and set the hook. It was the big one, at least three pounds. It made a run downstream and I followed. It stopped in the next hole and just stayed there. I put pressure on it and it began to move. I fought hard and finally, after at least ten minutes, I was able to guide it near the bank and I trapped it with my feet. I tossed my rod and used both hands and threw it up on the bank. It was a brown trout. I did not have a tape measure, but measured it with the handle of my fly rod. I guessed it was 18 ½ to 19 inches long.

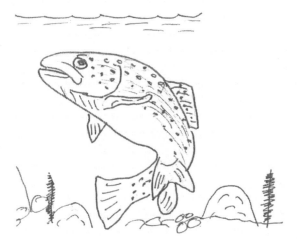

German Brown Trout

I used my needle nosed pliers to remove the number 6 hook. Brushed this big trout off in the water and took it back upstream and released it in the pine tree hole. It slowly swam off. That was exciting! I need to have Dad get me a landing net, not like Savannah's, but one like you might use in a lake. Besides Dad told me that if there is a threat of frost, the cranberry marsh upstream floods the berries to protect them. They pump most of the water back into the reservoir but some water is released downstream. When that happens the stream rises by eight to twelve inches and washes plenty of new food into the stream and the trout go on a feeding frenzy. I plan to fish the big sweep, the straight hole, the upstream sluice hole and the sluice dam hole if this flood of water occurs. Everything is wet from the rain, including me. The brush is wet so if I touch it I get wet. I changed clothes and hung my wet clothes up under the tarp. I hit the hay early. Savannah and her folks are coming to the camp tomorrow.

## June 11, 1948 - Early.

Heard the 'Beaver' running high all night. First thing this morning, the three foxes came to visit. I sat on my campstool and they came near. I got a slice of bread and tossed some pieces to them. They smelled of it and finally one of the pups ate one. The other two watched and then they went looking for some bread. I tossed two or three more and then I held one in my fingers. One danced around but all at once, it darted in and took the bread out of my fingers. It ran off a few feet and gulped it down. I held out another piece and this time two pups came after it. Finally, the bread was gone and I expected they might leave but no, they laid down about ten to twelve feet away. They all laid together in a heap and believe it or not, they went to sleep. As I sat there quietly, I saw a doe and two fawns moving toward camp. This family slowly climbed the small hill toward camp and finally, at about fifteen feet from the tent, realized something was different. The doe stopped and stamped one of her front feet. The fawns were on alert. When the doe stomped her foot it woke the foxes and they just looked at her and eventually went back to sleep.

The doe apparently felt no danger so she continued on past the tent. The fawns pranced around and butted heads. In about ten minutes this family moved out of sight to the north. About then I heard a cow moo in the distance. It sounded southwest of me. I did not realize that there were any cows nearby at all. Will have to check it out. Wonder if Savannah and her folks will come today with the high water. I hope they come.

## June 11, 1948 - Late.

Savannah and her parents do come.  I saw them coming downstream so I slipped down and waited by the stream.  They were intently fishing and I surprised them when I said hello.  They came up into the camp and were impressed with the set up.  I could only offer some logs to sit on.  Savannah's mom sat on the campstool, but we all hunkered down and visited.  I told them about the three foxes and the three deer and all the other critters I have seen or heard since I arrived in camp.  I explained that tomorrow afternoon my dad will drive a slow moving iron ore train going south and he will toss a bag to me and I will have another bag on a stick that he will grab.  This way I can keep getting food, clean clothes and other things and I can send dirty clothes, empty cans and notes about what I have been doing along with any requests for things I need the next week when Dad's train comes along.  We have agreed to only use the Friday train unless I need something from the Monday train.  I would need to send a note in the Friday sack that Dad picks up.

While we were sitting talking, three scarlet tanagers  came through the shrubs right up to the camp.  Boy those birds are really beautiful with their scarlet bodies and black wings.  As we sat there, Savannah's dad, Elon said, "Savannah has told us about the dugout.  I know you are planning to cut one limb and try to get into the dugout.  This is 1948 and whoever made the dugout may have owned the land it was on at one time.  The depression of the 1930s was not that long ago so I thought I could go to the court house in Shell Lake and go to the register of deeds, or land records, and see who owned that land.  It is possible that the owner could not pay the taxes and it reverted back to the county. The state wanted to create this Beaver Brook Wildlife Area so they may have bought that land from the county. I can tell by the plat book that the dugout must be close to the boundary of the wildlife area."

By now it was lunchtime and Savannah's mom, Kathy, said she had lunch for all of us. She produced ham sandwiches for all plus a bottle of Coca Cola for each. She also had chocolate chip cookies for dessert. Everyone really liked the campsite. The large white pines made a warm and friendly atmosphere. I told them they could come and spend a night with me any time, but there was only room for one more person in my tent. If they could bring another tent and mosquito netting they could spend the night. Perhaps catch enough trout for supper and the Casey's would provide additional food plus something for breakfast. We settled on this coming Saturday. They would plan on arriving by mid-afternoon.

We decided that there was enough day left that we should try to get into the dugout. We took my .22, the shovel, the saw and a flashlight and crossed the 'Beaver'. We took our hip boots off and put on shoes and headed to the dugout. In a few minutes, we came to the east side of the beaver pond. Savannah's mom and dad had never seen this pond. Savannah pointed out where the sticks were that we used to wade out to the deep spring hole. We did see a great blue heron wading along the south side of the pond. It was beautiful.

We arrived at the dugout and I crawled into the giant tree top and started sawing on the limb that seemed to be blocking our entry. I worked about fifteen minutes and finally sawed through the limb. Next I pushed it away enough to allow us to crawl into the dugout. I came out of the tree top and told Elon to take the flashlight and try to crawl in. He was bigger than me, but he slowly made his way in, first crawling over the limbs and then on his hands and knees. He disappeared in the dugout and the three of us waited. Finally after about five minutes, Elon appeared in the doorway and announced that it is quite a place in here. He told us to come on in.

The three of us took turns and made our way into the dugout. When I got inside and stood up, I saw that there were big log beams holding up the earth above. They were supported on each end by a stout upright timber. By the northwest wall stood a wood burning cook stove. On the opposite wall was a cot with remnants of a mattress on it. Near the remaining wall was a small table with one wooden chair by it. The doorway we crawled through had a heavy wooden door that swings inward. There were various pots, pans, coffee pot, plates, silverware, cups and other items sitting around or on a small shelf that sat on the floor which was dirt. There were plenty of spider webs and evidence that small animals had been in and out of the dugout. There was a gas lantern hanging from a nail on a ceiling beam along with about a dozen traps of various sizes.

Looking closer at the shelf on the ground, I shined the light toward the back of the bottom shelf and I could see a book there. I reached it and opened it and found if was a journal or diary of some sort. We decided to take it outside with us and we could look at it there. We saw an axe, shovel and saw standing near the stove. Whoever lived here either died or left in a hurry because they certainly didn't take many things with them.

We decided that we had seen enough and began to work our way under and over the giant tree top. When we got outside, we looked at the book and found entries on about 25 pages. No names but there were dates beginning with summer of 1928. That is when the dugout got finished. The last entry was fall of 1934, only 14 years ago. Elon seemed very interested in trying to find out who wrote the diary and who owned the property. He would like to take the book and seek out some of these answers. That was fine with me but I wanted to see it when he was finished with it. After we were finished, we should put it back. Maybe we should tell the Wisconsin Conservation Department about the dugout, provided it is on their Beaver Brook Wildlife Area property.

We decided to head back to the camp, but on the way we could follow the wheel tracks that I had followed when I found the trail that veered off to the dugout. We found the blue beech tree I had blazed and began to follow the ruts going southeast but before long they went south. As we followed the ruts, we passed the beaver pond just to its east. The ruts continued and we came to a well worn footpath. It ran east to west and must have disappeared after going a short distance to the west. We did not see a trail when we went to the dugout. I will have to follow that trail someday and see where it goes.

The ruts continued south but a small tamarack swamp stood in the way so the ruts turned to the west and went around the small swamp. We were to the point where Savannah and her folks needed to retrieve their fishing gear and hip boots and head for their car. I blazed a small ironwood tree so I would know where to start following the trail again.

We returned to their gear and they prepared to head to their car. We all agreed that it had been a fun day. Savannah followed her mom and dad and as she came past me she took my hand and leaned over and gave me a kiss on the cheek. WOW! That was the first kiss I had ever gotten from a girl and it was a zinger!!

Tonight I needed to build a fire to boil water. I crossed the 'Beaver', got my fly rod and some worms and headed for the rapids above the straight hole. The water was still high and it took me forty-five minutes to catch one 8 inch and two 8 ½ inch brookies. I did catch one horned dace which ended up on the bank. I cleaned the trout and headed to camp and got a fire started and started heating the water. I ate the trout, had bread and peanut butter and a small can of mixed fruit. That Savannah is beginning to really get my attention. She sure is nice.

**June 12, 1948 - Early.**

I will meet Dad and the train this afternoon. Moon is full, but came up late last night. The sky was clear and there were lots of fireflies. I heard what I think were night hawks last night. Not sure, but I think I heard a whippoorwill in the distance, also. The three foxes ran up from the south, but just ran around for awhile and then back to the south. Last night I heard the two tree frogs singing and I heard a high pitched song coming from the stream. I took the flashlight and followed the sound. There was a toad on the edge of the water. It puffed up a pouch of skin under its throat and let that air out and it makes that high pitched song. I watched and, low and behold, here comes another toad hopping along. It finds the one that is singing and tried to climb on it. They both go into the water and I can not see them. Must have wanted some privacy.

## June 12, 1948 - Late.

I decide to follow that trail that we found yesterday. I cross the 'Beaver' and take my hip boots off and put on shoes. It doesn't take long to find the trail and I follow it. It immediately goes up a big hill. I reach the top and it levels off. I had gone about 200 yards on the level when I looked ahead and could see people following the trail coming toward me. For what ever reason, I hunched down and ran to the south and got behind a small tip-up from a tree that had blown over many years ago. I was about 70 yards off the trail and could see three boys walking down the trail. They carried fishing poles, but were not wearing hip boots. They appeared to be about my age and older. They also seemed husky and were not real tall. They appeared to not have seen me. They also did not have fancy fishing gear and clothes so my guess is that they must live in the area, perhaps near where this trail leads.

I figured the three boys were going to fish on the stream, or the beaver pond, and would not be coming back on the trail for awhile. So I decided to continue following the trail to the east. After about a quarter of a mile I could see the forest was letting in more light so there must be an opening ahead. I continued and indeed did come to a road and across the road and a little to the north was a house. I could hear people talking and once a baby cried. My guess is that the three boys live in that house.

The road is a complete mystery to me. I did not know there was a road anywhere near me except what we drove in on when we went to the sand banks. I will have to ask Dad about the road and if he knows who lives there.

I wonder who those kids are. I don't want to talk to them as they may spill the beans about my camp. I decide to move south about 150 yards and go straight west until I run into the 'Beaver'. I could see I was coming to the edge of the big hill and, just as I was about to start down, my foot hit an old rusty can. I picked it up and wondered if there might be more old things nearby. Just to the north, I could see a depression and as I approached it, I could see a rusty barrel stove. The depression looked like someone had dug a shallow level spot for a small building, such as a hunting shack. There was no evidence of any wood structure, but there were lots of rusty cans, a pail, a pot and a coffeepot. This site was much older than the dugout. It appeared to be sized for only one or two people. I could picture a cozy, snug cabin maybe made out of logs perched on the edge of this big hill. Perhaps they hunted right out of the cabin and opened windows to shoot at deer. Maybe not.

I guessed that the 'Beaver' was only about 150-200 yards away. That would have been a source of water unless they had snow that they could melt. I took a stick and rooted around inside the outline of what I thought was the building. I found remains of a tin plate, several bottles, apparently for whiskey or such. I did find three rifle shells, .38-55 caliber. They had not been fired, but were very corroded.

This place either burned or it was built a long time ago, like 75 years because there is no sign of any of the wood used to build it. I check all the bottles for any date and on one I found 1877. Someone could have brought this bottle here long after 1877, but maybe not. I look at what is left of the barrel stove and, sure enough, on the casting for the door it said: Fireman, Milwaukee, 1873. My guess is that this place was built about 50 or more years ago.

I head for camp because I have to meet Dad's train at 4:47 p.m. I take my sack with empty cans, dirty clothes and letters to Mom and Dad with requests for a landing net and more flashlight batteries. I wait for the train and I can hear it signal a crossing just south of the switchyard. This train is very heavy. It is made up of ore cars carrying iron ore from the Mesabi Range to the Chicago area. Each car is about half the length of a regular box car. The track goes up hill from Spooner to Sarona, so there are three diesel engines on the front and two pushing from the rear.

They really roar, but only go about four to five miles per hour between Spooner and Sarona, which is about ten miles. At Sarona the two pushers disengage and come back to Spooner. They are barely idling because the track runs down hill. One windy day, the engineer looked out and saw three boys walking on the railroad tracks going north right into the wind. He realized that the boys could not hear the engines and they were very close to the boys. He blew the whistle and scared the boys and they jumped off on both sides of the tracks. Dad said that was a close call.

Finally, I see the engines, roaring as they slowly approach.

I had my bag rigged up on a large stick as Dad did not want me very near the engines. He dropped the bag for me fifty feet north of me. I held the bag up for him to grab as he leaned out the engine window. We both waved and I stood and watched Dad go away. I felt lonesome as I really missed both Mom and Dad. I gathered up my bag and headed toward camp.

I got to camp and opened the bag - Fried Chicken!! Wow! There is enough for breakfast, too. Four hardboiled eggs, more small cans of condensed milk, a loaf of fresh bread, cans of mixed fruit, oranges, apples, peanut butter, which she had already mixed up and put in syrup pail as dropping the glass jar that the peanut butter came in would break - maybe. There were about a dozen cookies and clean clothes. I ate half the chicken and an orange for supper. I went a distance and dug a hole for the chicken bones and orange peels. Tomorrow Savannah and her folks come to spend the night. Wonder how that will go? That Savannah seems to be on my mind a lot.

**June 13, 1948 - Early.**

Heard something sniffing around my tent last night. I also heard something climbing up a tree so took the flashlight and saw a raccoon climbing up the tree with my food bucket on it. I grabbed a stick and poked it and it came down the tree. I whacked it with the stick and hollered at it and I hope it got the message. Heard the tree frogs and the toads singing last night.

While eating breakfast I heard a catbird and saw an oriole. It hung around and sang its beautiful, loud song. It would be neat to have them build their hanging nest nearby. I buried my chicken bones and orange peels.

I hope this overnight with Savannah and her mom and dad goes OK. My guess is that Elon and I will sleep together and Savannah and her mom will sleep together. I put on clean clothes and wash up good. Mom sent some deodorant that I will put on. I wonder if Savannah will give me a kiss today. I sure hope so, but it is scary also. She sure is nice, though.

### June 13, 1948 - Late.

Can't write tonight - company.

### June 14, 1948 - Midday.

Savannah and her parents have left. Everything went very well. Elon had gone to Shell Lake to see who owned the property from 1928 to 1934. Land records showed that 40 acres, if it was the correct one, was owned by someone named Frank Steffan. The Register of Deeds document showed that indeed Mr. Steffan failed to pay the taxes for 1931, 1932, and 1933 so the county took possession at the end of 1934.

We discussed the dugout and Frank Steffan quite a bit. Elon had read some of the pages of his diary, if it was his. Apparently, he was a trapper and during the depression, the price of furs was so low that he had no way to pay his taxes and apparently not enough to buy food.

Elon and I did sleep in my tent. Savannah and her mom slept in the tent that they brought. That family does a fair amount of camping so they are used to the rustic life of a backwoods campsite. We talked about my family and they want to meet them someday. They seemed impressed that I would develop this campsite and spend the summer away from my friends in a lonesome environment. They admired my courage to do this adventure and wished me success for the rest of the summer.

Elon said, "There is a small stream that comes from the west and runs into this stream about 200 yards up stream. Do you know where it comes from?" "I didn't even know there was a stream there," I said. After breakfast, we decided to find the stream and follow it to its beginnings.

We stayed on the west side of the 'Beaver' and easily found the small stream. We also found three strands of barbed wire, which we crawled through. We followed the stream to the west and found lots of small pools with plenty of small brook trout. Several places the stream disappears under the tree roots for 20-30 feet. This little valley had many large pines, oaks and other trees. A train came by and we could see it above us as it crossed a trestle over the stream. This valley with its unusual little stream was spectacular. It presented a peaceful, quiet view in a tiny part of this huge woods.

The four of us continued and finally were under the trestle. We could see that cows had passed under this trestle, but not for a while. We looked to the northwest and we could see some buildings up on a hill, but we also could see that the cows were fenced out of the area we were in. Trees partially blocked the view of the buildings on the hill, but it looked like a barn, a house and maybe other buildings. There was an open field between the buildings and us and more of the field lay to the north. All of the field was on a large hillside.

We continued following this small, clear stream and after a short distance came to another fence. There appeared to be a pasture on the other side of the fence. The four of us held a short conference. We wanted to find the source of this stream as there may be a spring hole with trout in it. Finally we decided that Elon and I would follow the stream for a short distance. If we encountered any cattle, we would retreat.

Elon and I crossed the fence and followed the stream. The terrain was more level as the stream ran parallel to the railroad tracks. We did not see any cattle so we continued and came to a marsh of about seven to eight acres. This appeared to be the source of the stream and we decided that there didn't seem to be any spring hole with trout. We were about to go back to Kathy and Savannah when, all at once, it sounded like someone was pumping water with a hand pump. We both looked at each other. What is that? It sounded like it was fairly close by and was coming from the marsh. So we moved to the edge of the marsh and focused on the spot where the 'pumping' was coming from and finally we caught a slight movement and then we could see it. There was a good sized bird with striped feathers sitting with its beak straight up in the air. Elon thought it was one of the herons also called a 'shy poke'. It pumped several more times and then was silent. We were only about 25 feet from it and wondered if it was setting on a nest of eggs or babies.

We saw some cows to the southwest and decided that we should return to Kathy and Savannah and report what we saw. We decided that we should get back to camp as the Casey's had visitors coming by late afternoon.

We passed under the trestle which appeared to be 20 to 25 feet above the stream. We continued downstream following this rapidly falling, tumbling brook that played peek-a-boo with us as it disappeared under the roots for many feet. Kathy remarked that if she was a landscape artist, this would be a beautiful scene to paint.

We left the small stream and returned to camp. Elon reached in his pack and brought out the diary that we found in the dugout. He wanted me to have it and appreciated being able to look at it. He thought I would really enjoy its contents.

The Casey's said that they were going to take Savannah on a two week trip to visit Washington, D. C. and other places in the east. They would leave on June 15$^{th}$ and return about June 29$^{th}$ or 30$^{th}$. "Let's plan to meet you by the big pine hole at about 10:00 a.m. on Thursday, July 2$^{nd}$," said Elon. This sounded OK with me. I would miss Savannah, but it sure seemed like a wonderful trip. I hope Mom, Dad and I can do that trip next summer.

Elon, Kathy and Savannah put their hip boots on to cross the 'Beaver'. They gathered up the tent and other gear and said goodbye and headed out of camp toward the stream. I got an idea about then. "Do you know where you will be staying at Washington, D. C.?" I asked. Savannah knew it was a relative, but did not know the address. She asked her mom and she did not remember it just then. Savannah asked for my mom and dad's phone number because she would call them with the address when she got home tonight. "You could write a letter, send it with your dad and your mom could address it and put a stamp on it and drop it in the mail. I will send a letter to your folks address and your dad can deliver it with the Friday train. I will ask your mom for their address. Your mom and dad know about me, don't they?" "Oh, yes, they do," I said. Savannah held back and took my hand and leaned over and kissed me on the cheek! WOW!! That was another zinger! I had hoped a kiss might be possible, but - - I would be afraid to try to kiss her. Maybe someday.

### June 14, 1948 - Late.

Spent the day lying in camp, thinking about last night and this morning. Boy, Kathy provided great food both times. We spent the evening sitting around the fire pit, talking. Savannah's parents sure are smart. Both have lots of college training. Elon grew up at Drummond, Wisconsin and went to college at Superior State College in Superior. He specialized in biology. Kathy was raised on a farm by Birchwood, Wisconsin. She attended nurses training at Eau Claire State College in Eau Claire. They met when Kathy did her nursing training at Antigo, Wisconsin and Elon was teaching there.

Kathy's brother is a game warden in the counties east of Birchwood. She told many stories about following poachers in his car with the lights off. This happened many, many times. He also would wait for illegal beaver trappers and would crawl into a sleeping bag if it was cold. Many times he had to run the culprit down. Many times he took the person to a judge late at night to make the violator pay a fine or serve jail time. Apparently her brother is a very good game warden and he refers to himself as the 'Brush Cop'. When he has some time off his family and Savannah's family quite often get together as he has a cabin on the same farm property as Elon and Kathy. Kathy's mom and dad still live on the farm and do some farming. The men sometimes help with haying or other farm activities.

Savannah is in the junior high band and chorus at Antigo. She plays the clarinet in the band  She is planning to try out for band and chorus in high school at Antigo. She will be a freshman, like me, when school starts. Her school is much larger than mine, so competition is intense. Elon was a good basketball player and played in college. He encouraged me to give it a try. I think I will go out for the freshman team. I also am planning to try out for football. Need to have Mom or Dad find out when I need to report for equipment and practice.

**June 15, 1948 - Early.**

Hit the hay early last night.   Heard the owls and that is about all. I really slept good. I plan to read the trappers diary this morning. There are about 27 pages with writing on them, most pages I can read but some are difficult to read.

The first page tells about making the dugout in 1928. He did have a horse and a wagon to get his belongings hauled to the dugout. Later on - sold the horse and wagon for $125. Fall came and he shot a large buck. Scouted for his trap line. Figured he would set traps for beaver, mink, fox, raccoon, otter, muskrats and weasel. He had a tag for one timber wolf and one wildcat.

The trapping started after the first snowfall. The winter of 1928-29 had lots of snow and he had good luck on his trap lines. By the end of February he had 72 pelts stretched and drying in the dugout. We did not find anything that looked like it could be frames used to stretch various pelts. Perhaps he took them with him. He took his pelts to a buyer that he knew would pass through Spooner about March 15, 1929. He got paid $427. Beaver pelts were in demand. He went to Shell Lake and paid the tax on his 40 acres. $21 was what he owed.

Several times he wrote about walking to Spooner for supplies. He really liked fresh eggs and bacon. I wonder if he walked the railroad tracks or if there were trails that led to Spooner.

The fall of 1929, he worked at the cranberry marsh raking berries. Said he bunked at the marsh while he worked there.

The winter of 1929-30 he ended up with 76 pelts. The price was lower - got $403 for pelts. Paid tax of $26. Shot big buck. He shot lots of prairie chickens and ate well that winter - not so many eggs or bacon.

Summer of 1930 - he ate lots of blueberries, caught trout, and worked at cranberry marsh. He bunked at the marsh. The pay was less and the price of cranberries was down. Made $87.50. Winter 1930-31 very icy. It was a poor year trapping - only 46 pelts. The price way down, got $187. No trip to Shell Lake to pay tax, but maybe next year.  Shot a deer and many prairie chickens.  Hard, cold winter.

Summer 1931 there were lots of fires.  None real close to his dugout - about one mile away.  Dry, hot spring.  No blue berries - not much cash for supplies - cooked  lots of cornbread.  He worked at the cranberry marsh most of the summer, bunked there and made $173.50.  Raked cranberries in the fall and earned $76.25.

Winter of 1931-32 - very little snow, icy and poor trapping conditions plus another trapper in his territory.  He ended up with 43 pelts and got $151.  No trip to Shell Lake to pay taxes.  Finally shot a deer and only a few prairie chickens.  He applied for job with railroad,  may be some watchman work.

Summer 1932.  Hot and dry.  Some fires but not as bad as last year.  Work part time as watchman for railroad.  Get $28.75 per month.  Raked cranberries on certain days and made $71.50.

Trapping season 1932-33 - good conditions.  Lots of snow ended up with 57 pelts.  Price is poor and he got $141.50.  No tax this year.  He  expects to  lose this 40 acres and this dugout. In the spring he got a visit from the sheriff.  He has  warned him that if he didn't pay back tax of $86 plus interest the county will seize this 40 acres by the end of 1934.   He told the sheriff he would try, but this depression is really brutal. The sheriff was nice about the whole thing.  He has been very busy as many, many people are in the same shape he is in - or worse. Already lots of farms and businesses have been lost to creditors.  Very few jobs.  Besides the summer weather has been very hot and dry.  Several fires this spring.

He got a job on the railroad rip track crew.  This is full time.  They work out of Spooner and take hand cars to work.  He still lives in the dugout, but makes enough pay so he will look for a room in Spooner.  He will not trap this winter and hopes he can afford room  and board out of his pay.  Still has the $125 from selling the horse and wagon.  He  could pay back tax, but he has very little use for the land if he lives in town.  He will try to get his things out of the dugout before the end of December.

His years of living in the dugout, trapping, hunting and working at the cranberry marsh were good.  Times got too hard so it was time to move on.  He will be 32 years old soon and he said he will miss the dugout.

That was the end of writing in the diary.  Wow!  I did not realize that times during the depression were so hard for so many people.   My dad had steady work with the railroad and I was born in 1934, apparently in the deepest part of the depression.  By the time I was six years old, the depression was over and World War II was about to start.  Actually World War II had a much greater impact on my life than the great depression did.  I really was unaffected by the events of the 1930s.  Most of my friends fathers worked for the railroad also and it appears that work on the railroad must have been fairly steady.   For people to lose their job and then lose their house or business must have been very hard.  What did they do for food? And a place to live?

I did hear my dad talk about government projects to improve and protect trout streams from erosion.   When we fished Sawyer Brook, Dad said that stream was worked on by many, many men and teams of horses. Apparently projects like that provided jobs for many people. Thinking back on school, I think the TVA was developed in the 1930s. It seems like one of the big dams out west was built in the 1930s. More than likely there were many projects sponsored by the government. The 1930s must have been very difficult for most people.

**June 15, 1948 - Late.**

I spent an hour watching the straight hole. I did see one large trout, maybe over three pounds. Wonder what I should write to Savannah. I really like her, but I don't know what I should say. I also don't want Mom or Dad to read it, but I don't have any envelopes so I will have to write the letter and then have Mom put it in an envelope to be mailed to Savannah. Wish Dad would drop off envelopes when his train goes by tomorrow afternoon. Sure wish I could call Mom and ask her to send envelopes but - no phone out here.

Heard a strange sounding bird and went looking for it. I saw it and am pretty sure it was a cuckoo. Just before dark the doe and her two fawns came walking by the tent. They stopped about 75 feet away and the two fawns decided it was time to eat, so they both started sucking from the same side and their little tails were really wagging. That went on for about five minutes and then they continued going south and were out of sight in a few minutes.

## June 16, 1948 - Early.

I heard the owls last night. Also heard some kind of howl far away. Heard night hawks and smelled a skunky smell so maybe the mink was around last night. So far, the only time any animal has tried to get at the food bucket hanging from a rope was one raccoon.

Today I want to walk the railroad tracks going south. I want to see the cranberry marsh and, if possible, see the reservoir. Dad said it would be a little over a mile down the track from my trail going to camp. Have to get back to meet Dad's train by 4:47 this afternoon. I packed a peanut butter sandwich and headed out at 8:30 a.m.

## June 16, 1948 - Late.

I met Dad's train and he had a sack for me and it had envelopes and stationery in it!!!! Wow, that puts my mind at ease a little. I still am worried about what I should write to Savannah. It was good to see Dad if only to wave at him and say hello as his engines slowly passed making a huge roar because the very heavy load of iron ore. These iron ore trains began running during WWII as more iron was needed to make tanks, trucks etc. for the war.

I have always enjoyed walking the railroad tracks. The ties are spaced so it takes a giant step to skip one tie. If I step on each tie, I take baby steps. So eventually I do what most kids do and that is to balance on the rail and see how far I can go. It seems that there are interesting things to see along the tracks. Because you can walk quietly, it is possible to see some wild life.

I could really see the buildings up on the hill that we could see from under the trestle. A few hundred feet further south put me next to an open field on the west side of the tracks. I could also get a glimpse of the marsh where the shy poke was 'pumping water'. On the east side of the tracks were many giant white pines and other large oak trees.

Several hundred feet further south, I could see a dirt road running beside the tracks. Could this be the road I found a few days ago with the house near it? My gut feeling is that it was the same road. A few hundred feet further and I could see the beds and channels of the cranberry marsh off to the southeast. I could see workers and equipment out on the dikes by the channels. I look to the south of the beds and see what must be a dam. My guess is that the reservoir is behind that dam so I follow the road that leads to the dam. I realize that I am on private property but hope I won't get into any trouble.

I arrive at the dam and indeed it holds back a large lake of water. I can see old stumps sticking out of the water in places, but the long dam holds back an enormous amount of water. I can see a small building and I look in it and see a huge engine attached to a very large pump in a large pipe about two feet in diameter that leads back into the reservoir. That must be how they pump most of the water back into the reservoir when they have to flood the berries to prevent frost damage. My guess is that if there is threat of frost, the entire maze of beds to the north of the reservoir is flooded until the frost danger is past. Water is then pumped back behind the dam to be used again.

I can see clams imbedded in the sand with just their

siphons showing. I wonder if there are any fish in these waters. About then, two boys on bikes rode up with casting rods over their handle bars. I moved toward the east side of the dam and stopped about at the halfway mark. I threw stones and pretended to not pay any attention to the boys who appeared to be about my age, or younger. They began casting off the dam near the gate and in a few minutes, one boy caught a nice long fish which I guessed was a northern pike. It must have weighed two or three pounds. I guess that answered the question about fish being in these waters.

The boys moved to the southwest and were fishing off another gate used to flood beds to the west of the lake. I saw this as my chance to get off the dam and head back to camp. A few hundred feet from the dam I could see a crew of workers near the road ahead. I saw that I could take a short road that joined the dirt road that ran along the tracks. I took this route and came to two small shacks. I noticed two Indians sitting outside of one shack, one was a young man and the other was a young woman. The shack was quite close to the road and I had to walk close to them and they both said hello and I responded. They both got up from their chairs and came to talk to me. They were very pleasant and friendly. I was a little scared, as this was the first time I had ever talked to any Indian. I had seen the Hayward Indians put on their pow-wow at Spooner, but this was different.

They wanted to know my name, which I told them it was Nick. They told me their names. She was Little Dove and he was Walking Bear. They said that they work at the marsh, but today was a day off for them. I asked if they fished off the dam and they said they did and they catch nice northern, which they eat. They also catch trout out of the stream further to the north. I asked if they stayed all winter and they said no. When the berries are done, they catch a train and go to Alabama for the winter.

About that time, a fast moving passenger train came through and I was reminded that I better get going. Little Dove said they were just going to fix some lunch and wanted me to join them. I was very uneasy about going into the shack with them so I told them that I really needed to get going. I said goodbye and continued down the road. They invited me to stop again, and I said I would, even though I was pretty certain that I wouldn't. I had just turned the corner and was still near the shack when Little Dove said, "Wait, I have something for you." She went around on the road and had something in her hand. "I want you to have this because it could bring you luck. Also, it will be a reminder of our meeting today." She handed me the gift and it was a rabbits foot with a beaded strap on it. It was very nice and I thanked her for it. She said she made it and likes to give them to people that she likes and she said, "I like you." Now, I was blushing. She reached out and put her hand on my arm and thanked me for stopping to visit with Walking Bear and her.

Finally, I was able to continue walking, but I felt a strong urge to spend more time with this couple. I had not eaten my sandwich yet, so I looked for a spot and saw where Beaver Brook ran out of the maze of cranberry beds. There was a small bridge over the stream so I went and sat down on a large rock under the bridge. As I ate my sandwich, I heard two kingfishers make their distinctive song. There was a sand cliff on the west side of the stream and at least a couple dozen cliff swallows had burrowed into the sand and made nests. The adults were busy catching bugs out of the air and taking them to the babies in the tunnels. All at once, one of the kingfishers flew down and dove into the stream about fifteen feet from me. Very shortly it emerged out of the water with a small minnow in its mouth. It flew out of my sight so it may be going to its nest to feed babies, also.

As I sat there finishing my sandwich, I saw a strange animal come to the stream to get a drink. It was only about 18 or 20 feet away. I could see it clearly. I guessed immediately that it was a weasel. It was brown and about eighteen inches long with short legs. The weasel has a reputation as a nasty killer and its pelt turns white in winter and is called ermine.

I finish my sandwich and get back on the railroad track, just in time to step off as a long freight train goes north. It was being pulled by a steam engine as apparently the diesel locomotives are replacing the steamers. There is a huge difference in the sound of their whistles. I prefer the steam engine whistle.

As I walk back to my camp, I go around a curve on the tracks and far down they curve to the right. Just beyond that curve I can see the buildings of that farm that was near the trestle. It is on a large hill and I can hear car and truck noise as vehicles go up this large hill. It must be the hill with the 'Hilltop Cabins' on it. I figure out that the farm must be close to the eight cabins that travelers use that are on top of the hill. I can see some cows on the big field just west of the tracks so there must be a farm around here also. I know there is a big field very close to where I meet Dad's train so there must be a farm near there.

I got back to camp by late afternoon and realize I need to get a fire going tonight, so I must catch enough trout for supper. I dig some worms out of my stash and, with hip boots, creel and fly rod, head for the sluice dam and the meadow curve hole. I have not fished these holes yet.

As I approach the sluice dam, I try to picture men building this dam, filling it with water and then opening the gates to let this huge surge of water carry the winters pine log cutting to a faraway sawmill. I ease into the water above the four 12" x 12" timbers that span the stream and are partially submerged. I already know that there are two nice undercuts on the west side between the first and second timbers and also between the third and fourth timbers. My worm had barely been in the water between one and two timbers when I felt a very solid hit. I was not able to do much with the fish, but in a few seconds it swam to the east between the timbers. I could not hold it and it went under number two and back to the west. My line got snagged on the timbers and I had to put my rod tip in the water to get unengaged. I was able to finally tire this nice trout out, but it was between timber two and one and the water was over my hip boots. I had not brought my landing net so, now what?

The trout was completely tired out and I was able to keep it on top of the water, so I decided to shorten the grip on my fly rod and pull the trout to me and grab it by the jaw.

I moved slowly and was able to finally do that even though my left hand with the fly rod was far behind me.

The trout was a real beauty and had swallowed the hook. It was a 14 ½ inch brook trout and it was very colorful with its distinctive spots. This would be plenty of supper for me, so I was done fishing for today. I returned to camp and got a fire going to sterilize water to drink and also to fry this nice trout.

Brook Trout

After supper, I tried to write a letter to Savannah. After a couple starts that ended up in the fire, I decided to tell her what I did yesterday and today. Since I still had two more days before meeting Dad's train, I knew I may have more to add so I stopped writing and just sat by the fire. I feel that I am beginning to grow up. I feel good about the wonderful world I see around me. I admire all the different plants and animals I see and am impressed with the great variety of vegetation. I am pleased with all the wildlife I have seen so far. I wonder about the three foxes

- I have not seen them for a few days. I hear the bird I think is a cuckoo again tonight. So far the mosquitoes and deer flies have not been as bad as I know they can be. I have picked about a dozen wood ticks off me and I check several times a day. I certainly don't want them to puff up as big as I have seen them on dogs ears. Tomorrow I will get started on my book I was going to write. Hope I get a premonition about what it will be about.

## June 17, 1948  - Early.

I heard two owls last night. The owls were very close. There must be at least three of them. I heard rustling this morning and looked out and saw the three foxes. I went out and sat on my stool. All three came very close. I held my hand out and one came up and smelled it and then gave it a lick. It sat down and I leaned out to touch it, but it moved away. These foxes sure are curious. They sniff everything and one even stuck his head into the tent. One must have heard a mouse because, all at once, it pounced on something in the leaves and immediately the other two were right there to see what the first one caught. It held it under its paws and slowly got its mouth down to where the mouse, or whatever, was trapped and sure enough there was a mouse. The half grown foxes didn't quite know what to do with the mouse so it got away only to be pounced on by a different fox. This time, the fox actually had the mouse in its mouth as the other two tried to get it away. The fox with the mouse actually figured out that the mouse was good to eat and it began to eat it. The other two came and tried to get some of the mouse, but they could not get the mouse away from the fox who had it. Before long it was all eaten.

I did not get a premonition about what I could write a book about. Many possible topics cross my mind, but I am not knowledgeable in many subjects, so I don't really have anything to write about. Maybe it could be about a fourteen year old boy camping alone in the big woods.

I decide to cross the 'Beaver' and explore up on the big hill to the east of the stream. I am still curious as to who lives in the house on the dirt road. I make a peanut butter sandwich and put on my hip boots to cross the 'Beaver'. I will change into my shoes and stash the hip boots until I return.

## June 17, 1948 - Late.

Covered plenty of woods today. I went to the top of the big hill to the east and went straight north. After about one mile I came to the edge of the woods. Found where loggers had cut some large oak trees and they drug them out so trucks coming off the dirt road could carry them away. This had been done one or two years earlier. I could look across the dirt road and see the top of a barn just over a hill. I will have to explore that sometime. I wonder where this dirt road comes out? I headed south until I came to the foot path and took that down to the stream. No sign of the kids today. It was quite warm and I worked up a sweat today.

## June 18, 1948 - Early.

Today I will go north and stay to the west of the meadows. I plan to go to the sand banks and then come back on the west bank of the 'Beaver'. The three foxes came running up as I was getting ready to leave. I sat on the stool and watched their antics. They circled the tent. And apparently they must have heard something in the leaves as all three had their noses about two inches off the ground and at the same spot. One finally pawed that spot and he uncovered a salamander. This amphibian was a complete mystery to the pups. They watched it crawl under the leaves and made no attempt to uncover it or try to catch it.

## June 18, 1948 - Late.

Long day. It was hard walking on the west side of the meadows. I found several blow-downs that formed a shelter of sorts. These were spruce trees that apparently blew over twenty years or so ago. I was curious so I made my way into what looked like an opening to a den or a place to seek shelter. I got to the opening and could not see much inside because it was too dark. There did appear to be a room-like place where an animal would be out of the weather. I will bring my flashlight and get a better look at what is inside. Need to catch some trout and sterilize water tonight. Went to the big sweep hole and floated a worm very near the overhanging bank. The first pass produced a nice nine inch brookie. A few feet further downstream produced a nine inch brown trout. Fishing has been fantastic. I get a fire going, fry the trout and boil water.

## June 19, 1948 - Late.

Yesterday I had just finished eating supper when I heard a loud splash coming from the 'Beaver' about 75 yards to the north. In a few seconds I heard a woman's voice call for help. I immediately ran towards the sounds and got to the stream and found a middle aged woman sitting in the stream in water up to her shoulder. She said, "I smelled your campfire and skirted around where I thought the fire was and came back to the stream and slid into it to fish for a few more minutes. The water was deeper than I expected and besides I got my left foot hooked on a root and I fell in the water. I also felt a sharp pain in my left leg and now I can't stand up."

I kicked off my shoes and socks and waded in to help her out of the water. She still had her fly rod in her hand. I really didn't know how I was going to help, but thought I'd better try. First, she handed me her fly rod and I put that on shore. She told me she was from near Birchwood and her name was Margaret Burns. I went behind her and tried lifting under her arms. I was careful as I certainly did not want to hurt her anymore. I lifted and she helped with her right leg. She was able to stand up, but her left leg really was painful. She put her left arm around my neck and I put my right arm around her waist and we slowly made our way out of the stream. We paused to rest and then continued toward camp where I told her we could dry off her clothes by the fire.

It took about 25 minutes to reach the campsite. Now what? I already found out that her car was back by the bridge which was a good mile upstream. The sun was already very low so it would be impossible to get to her car and a hospital tonight. Margaret understood and agreed that she would need to spend the night in my camp, probably in the tent.

I thought we could dry her clothes out by morning when I would help her get to her car. I put more wood on the fire and told Margaret that she needed to get the wet clothes off so they could be dried. She could put on some of my clothes in the meantime. I went into the tent and found a pair of socks, a pair of pants and a shirt and gave them to Margaret. I helped take off her socks and then I turned away so she could take off the wet clothes and put on the dry ones. In a few minutes she had changed clothes.

I asked if she was hungry and she reluctantly said she was. I asked if she had caught any trout and she said she had caught four 8" to 9" inch trout. I offered to fix them for her plus a slice or two of bread and an orange. She was very willing to allow me to fix the trout. I could see lots of pain on her face from her injured leg. I helped her to sit down on the camp stool. That was a difficult thing to do and I was worried about getting her up off the stool and eventually into the tent.

I fixed the trout and she ate them and the bread but could not do the orange. I had already begun drying her clothes by the fire. I had a bottle of aspirin and offered those to her. She gratefully accepted some and hoped they would take effect soon. She also asked if I could massage her left leg and see if that helped.

I began squeezing and gently rubbing near her knee. From her reaction, the more painful part was from in front of below her knee and above the knee and in front of the leg. Margaret said her leg really felt better as I massaged it.

I poured water out of her hip boots and pushed towels down into the toes of each boot. From time to time, I took the towels out and dried them by the fire. The dry towels were shoved back into the boots to dry them out.

By now it was dark and I told Margaret that we needed to get her into the tent and on the cot so she could stretch the knee out and, hopefully, get some sleep.

I got the cot ready and went behind her and lifted as she also pushed up. Slowly we got her standing again and step by slow step got her to the tent where I helped her to sit on the cot first and then turn around and lie down. All this took great effort and I could see lots of pain in her face.

She asked me to massage her leg again, which I did for about ten minutes. By then, she had her eyes closed and seemed ready to fall asleep. I went out and tended to drying her clothes and hip boots.

By now, I had time to come up with an idea about getting Margaret to her car and to a hospital. Early in the morning, we would eat breakfast and Margaret would put her dry clothes back on. We would put hip boots on and cross the 'Beaver'. She would take off her hip boots and wait while I went to her car by the bridge. I would take her hip boots, fly rod and creel also. I would bring back her shoes or boots and we would begin the long slow trip to her car.

After about two hours, she called to me and asked if I could give her two more aspirin and massage her leg again. I gave her the aspirin and started squeezing and massaging her leg while I told her about my plan. She thought the plan sounded good and she agreed to it. What happens after we get to the car? I told her I had not thought about that yet. The aspirin had apparently begun to take affect by this time. I had worked on her leg for about 15 minutes.

I got a little sleep, but I really wanted those clothes to get dry by morning so it took constant attention. After a couple more hours, Margaret called to me and wanted me to massage her leg again. I began squeezing and massaging her leg. She said it still hurt, but the massaging made it feel better. I asked her if she was going to see a doctor or go to the hospital. She said she really needed to at least see a doctor. I asked here where her doctor was? Was it in Spooner, Rice Lake or Shell Lake. She said she was going to a doctor in Spooner.

I asked if she would be able to drive her car and she said, "No, because it has a clutch and a standard transmission. And since my left leg doesn't work, I will not be able to drive." She asked me, "Can you drive me to Spooner?" "What kind of car is it?" I asked. "A 1937 Ford," was her answer. "That is the same car as my dad has," I said, "but I really have only driven it out in a field. Maybe you could tell me how to shift and whatever else I need to know."

I went back to the fire to tend the clothes. Today is Friday and I need to finish writing my letter to Savannah and get it and other things to my dad's train by 4:47 p.m. I can see that it may take several hours to get Margaret from the camp to the car. I would have to walk the railroad tracks from Spooner to my camp to get the letter and my bag of things to return to Mom.

The clothes were nearly dry. I can see a little light on the eastern horizon. Margaret has apparently been sleeping for about three hours. I let the fire burn itself out. I rustle up some breakfast for us. Cheerios, condensed milk and oranges. Margaret wakes up and I offer her two more aspirin. She wants me to massage her leg again, which I do. I tell her about my schedule today and say we need to get going early.

We eat breakfast and I bring her dry clothes into the tent. She changes back into her clothes and is ready for some help getting up off the cot. I bend over her and she put her arm around my neck. I put my hands on her waist and we both lift and push and up she came. She said thank you and gave me a hug. Margaret is slender, pretty and reminds me of my mom. I can see that the pain is intense but she seems brave about it.

In a few minutes she announces that she will need help getting the hip boots on. I help her and in a few minutes she is ready to go.

I take the camp stool and Margaret puts her left arm around my neck and I put my right arm around her waist and we hobble down the incline to the stream. I picked a spot where there was rapids and a manageable bank to step down and up. It was tricky, but we eventually made it. I asked if she wanted aspirin and she said yes. I went back to camp and got aspirin and water for her.

We both took off our hip boots and Margaret sat on the camp stool. I took her hip boots, fly rod and creel and said goodbye. I headed for her car parked by the bridge at least one mile away, maybe farther.

I follow the trail by the stream and in about a half hour, I arrive at her car. I stash the rod, boots and creel in the brush in case someone comes by and wants some nice gear. I find her shoes in the car and take them as I head back to Margaret waiting on the campstool.

About a half hour later I get back to Margaret and she is happy to see me. I help her put her shoes on and once again she puts her arms around my neck and my hands on her waist and up she comes. It takes a few seconds to steady herself, but I grab the foot stool in my left hand, put my right arm around her waist and she puts her left arm around my neck. Away we go at a snails pace. Right off, I see a major problem. The trail was made by people walking single file, not side by side.

We plug along and rest about every 20-25 minutes. It is not long and we are by the big pine hole. Margaret said she caught a plump 15 inch brookie there yesterday and released it after she measured it. She was sure she saw a much larger trout while she fought the fish she caught.

As we slowly ambled along, I asked her if she fished the 'Beaver' often. She said that yesterday was her first time. I asked, "Why did you choose this stream?" She said, "I met a family from over by Birchwood that were avid trout fishermen, as I am. They recommended this beautiful stream and said they were going to take their daughter and go to Washington, D. C. for a couple weeks and suggested that I fish it once while they were gone." I asked Margaret if she knew the name of their daughter. She said, "Yes, and the parents are Elon and Kathy Casey." Wow! What a coincidence. I decided to play dumb about the whole thing.

After resting at the big pine hole, we started out again. We were at least halfway and the sun was fairly high. I guessed 9:30 or 10:00 a.m. Margaret was getting tired and her leg was hurting big time. I sure hope nothing is broken. We came to one fairly sharp hill to climb and it was really a challenge but we made it. I heard a car go by so I knew we were getting close to the road and the bridge. By now, Margaret held on to me with both arms and I really had to lift her to keep moving. We finally arrive at the dirt road and I decided to let her rest on the camp stool while I go get the car and her gear. She gives me the key and asked if I knew how to drive and I stammered some and finally said no.

"My dad has a car just like yours and I have steered it and shifted some, out in a field." I said. She laughed and gave me a short lesson about starting the car. Next came the use of the clutch on the left and the shifting lever. The brake pedal and the gas pedal were discussed and off I went as the car was about 100 yards southwest of our location.

I found her gear and put it in the 1937 Ford. I put the key in the ignition and pushed the clutch in and turned the key. In a couple of seconds the engine fired up. I ground the gears, but by looking on the knob of the gear shift, I could tell where reverse was. I slowly let the clutch out and the car died. Now what? I tried starting again and it fired up. This time I gave it more gas and when I let the clutch out, the car shot backward and I jammed on the brakes and I stopped in the middle of the dirt road. Wow, that was close, because there is a steep bank behind the car and Beaver Brook runs there.

There was just enough room for me to shift into first and turn sharply and head up the hill to pick up Margaret. I did dig up the gravel when I took off, but I made it! I pulled up by Margaret and she was laughing. I put the brake on, got out and asked her what she was laughing at. She said she could barely see me behind the steering wheel and she heard me dig up the road when I started. But she said she was really happy that I had gotten the car by her so she could go to the doctor. I bent over her and she put her arms around my neck. I lifted and she pushed and up she came. This time she hung on to me and gave me a big kiss. She said she really appreciated all that I had done to help her. I helped her into the car and felt my legs were a little queasy. Maybe that kiss affected me or I could be tired from our long slow walk.

I got in and shifted into first gear. I was going to be content to stay in that gear on this road. I just wanted to get Margaret to Spooner. It wasn't long and we came to a steep, rocky hill. I got about halfway up the hill and started spinning the tires on all the small rocks. Now what? I stepped on the brakes and realized that I needed to back down the hill and get a run at it. So I did what I saw my dad do. I opened the door, leaned out and looked backward and let the car roll down the hill. We got to the bottom and now I realized that I needed to put the car in reverse and back up far enough to get a run at the hill. This meant I would have to shift into second and floor the gas pedal. I asked Margaret if that is what we needed to do and she suggested that I could start out in $2^{nd}$ gear to avoid shifting on the go. She said, "Try it and if it doesn't work, you can start over again."

I put the car in $2^{nd}$ gear, revved the engine and let the clutch out and away we went. This time the car had much greater speed and we went up the hill with a few rocks flying but we made it. Margaret cheered!! I slowed down because we had to go down the other side of this hill and I could see a big water hole on one side of the road. Just beyond the water I could see another good sized hill so I needed to keep the speed up around the water hole so we could get up the hill. I told Margaret to 'hang on' as we went around the east side of the water. I hit the gas pedal and we started up the next hill. A few rocks flew, but we made it. When we got to the top of the hill, I could see the big house I had seen from the trail. I also could see two or three people around the house.

We continued north and in about one-half mile we started down a long hill. I could just see the top of a barn to the east side of the road. We made it to the bottom of the hill and in a short distance came to a sharp curve to the right and then another curve to the left. Next was a long gradual hill. I could see two farms to the west of the road. The road entered some woods and was curvy. In a while we could see a stop sign so I slowed down and stopped. Maybe this would be a good time to tell Margaret about the rest of my plan and hoped it was OK with her.

I told her that I was trying to keep my camping out this summer a secret to the people in Spooner. I needed to meet the train my dad drove by about 4:47 and it was 1:30 now. I want to stop the car at the auto body shop just before we cross the railroad tracks. I would stick my head in the door and tell them that you need to get to the doctor. I would run to the railroad tracks and head back to my camp as I need to get things put together to give to Dad. I did not want to be seen and hoped the people at the auto body shop won't recognize me and I won't meet anyone on the tracks. Margaret felt very bad that I would have to be so secretive on her account. She wondered if there could be another way. Then she realized that since she could not drive the car, there were not many options. She also didn't want me to be seen and have other people find out about my snug campsite in the forest by the stream.

Before we started on to Highway 70, Margaret leaned over and gave me another big kiss and thanked me for all I had done to help her. We drove onto the highway and after about two miles came into Spooner. I pulled the car up in front of the auto body shop and shut the engine off. I went into the office and kept my head turned. I told one of the men that there was a lady in the '37 Ford with an injured leg. Could someone drive her to the doctor? With that, I ran out, grabbed the camp stool and ran to the railroad tracks about 150 feet away. I did not look back and ran south down the tracks across the trestle and before long I was out of sight from anyone at the auto body shop. I eventually got out of town and began walking.

I sure hope Margaret gets to the doctor alright. She sure seemed like a very nice lady. I really felt sorry for her being in such pain. I wonder if I will ever see her again. She does know the Casey's, and said she knows Savannah. That reminded me that I needed to finish my letter to Savannah so Mom can mail it after Dad gets home.

I did finally reach camp by 3:30 p.m. I finished the letter to Savannah and mentioned that I met Margaret Burns near my camp. I wrote about the fishing and that

Margaret caught a 15 inch brook trout at the big pine hole and released it. I mentioned the three foxes coming in to camp and then signed it, Nick, but I put an X under my name. I sealed the envelope and put it in the bag with the dirty clothes, empty cans and a list of things I needed as Mom and Dad were planning on visiting camp Sunday afternoon.

I got up to the tracks just in time to hear the train slowly pulling its load of iron ore. I wave at Dad and he drops his bag. I have my bag on the stick and Dad grabs it. In a few minutes he is out of sight so I pick up my bag of goodies and head back to camp. I will hit the hay early as I am really tired and sore from helping Margaret reach the car. I wonder if Margaret is in the hospital. I wonder if she is married, or has any kids. We did not talk about that at all. I certainly hope she is not hurt very bad. She did seem like a very nice lady, very much like my mom.

The three fox pups came into the camp briefly but went back to the south.

**June 20, 1948 - Noon.**

I slept like a log. I was really tired. I still feel stiff and sore from helping Margaret to her car from my camp. I hear voices and can see two people with fly rods near the stream. In a few minutes they are out of sight to the north of me. I ate a very late breakfast and decide to crawl back into my tent and sleep.

**June 20, 1948 - Late.**

I woke up about 3:00 p.m. Decided to look for a den the

three half grown foxes still call home. I head southeast looking for hillsides where mother fox could make a den. I searched for about an hour and all at once the three foxes jumped up from a spot, close to me, and ran off toward the southeast. I called to them, which had no affect. I stood still and in about five minutes they came back, sniffing cautiously. I sat down on the ground and eventually all three pups came very close and one sniffed my hand and gave it a lick. All three circled around and after a few minutes they laid down in a heap about eight feet from me. In about ten minutes they were sleeping. My guess was that the den for these foxes must be nearby. I didn't want to wake the sleepers, but from my position I could not see a den.

After about 20 minutes, I stood up. I took a couple steps toward the south and the foxes woke up and got up, but didn't run away. They let me walk away about twenty feet and then all three began following me. I kept looking for a den and finally on the south side of a hummock there was a den. The opening was very well used. I think by this stage in these three foxes lives, they don't go in the den much anymore, but they don't get very far away either. While I waited, a pileated woodpecker flew to a dead aspen tree and started pecking. This woodpecker really made the chips fly when it found a promising spot for a worm or two.

I realize that I am very close to the small stream that flows under the trestle. I found the stream and sat near one of the larger pools. I could see several brook trout zipping around in the pool. The largest was about 8 inches long. While sitting there, I heard a twig snap south of me. I watched and in a few minutes I could see the outline of a deer coming toward me. In a few minutes I could see that it was a buck with a beautiful rack that was still in the velvet. The deer seemed to be headed in my direction so I just sat quietly and watched. The buck kept coming and finally stopped by the pool I was sitting by and took a drink of water. I was about twelve feet away and the buck was apparently not aware of me. It got through drinking and raised its head and looked around. I could easily count the points on his antlers and there were ten. I estimated that his antlers were at least 20 inches wide. The buck turned toward the east and slowly ambled away, apparently completely unaware that I sat so close to it. That was a very impressive animal. I can see why hunters get 'buck fever' at the sight of a nice buck. I can hardly wait to tell Dad about this beauty. After all, Dad and I hunted here last deer season so if he knows there is this ten pointer here, he may want to hunt here again. I know I would want to, but after seeing this beautiful animal, I might have a hard time trying to shoot it. I ate a can of Spam for supper.

## June 21, 1948 - Early.

Mom and Dad come today. Wonder if they will have a letter from Savannah. I hope so. Mom has put the last weeks Spooner paper in my bag and I read it all. This morning for the first time, two red squirrels came down one of the big pine trees. They scurried around for a few minutes and then went back up one of the big pines.

## June 21, 1948 - Late.

Mom brought fried chicken and it was outstanding. She made enough for me to eat for supper also. There was a letter from Savannah. I waited and opened it after Mom and Dad left. It had SWAK on the back of the envelope. What is SWAK? She sent it from Gettysburg, Pennsylvania. She and her folks visited the battlefield where a great Civil War battle was fought. Savannah was very impressed with the hundreds of thousands of troops that fought there and how many died or were wounded. It made a tremendous impact on her. She wrote that they would be at their relatives house near Washington, D. C. by Thursday and will tour the Capitol, White House, three big memorials and Arlington National Cemetery. She hoped to get a letter from me soon.

I told Mom and Dad about the big buck. Dad was excited about that. I also told about Margaret Burns falling in the stream and hurting her leg. I related the entire story including me driving her '37 Ford into Spooner. They both laughed when I told about not being able to get up the hill the first time. They also were impressed that I figured out a plan to help Margaret without giving myself away. I asked if they could try to see if she had a telephone number as she lives near Birchwood. Maybe you could call her and see how she is and then tell me. You would not have to tell your name. Mom said she would try to contact her and let me know.

Mom seems more at ease in the camp today. Apparently, she thinks her little boy is doing just fine and probably doesn't have to worry about me. It was really a great afternoon with Mom and Dad. They had brought two camp stools so we all could sit in some comfort. They will leave the stools with me. Mom saw Ellen, one of my classmates, at the store and she asked about me. Mom told her that I was staying at her brothers ranch in Montana. Ellen is a girl that seems very nice. I did dance with her three times at a school dance last spring. She seems interested in me and is in my grade. Maybe we will be in some classes together. I like Ellen, but I find myself thinking about Savannah lots of times. I definitely am looking forward to meeting her by the big pine on July 2nd.

I told Dad about finding the tangle of uprooted trees on the west side of the meadows. I said I was planning to take my flashlight and explore that cave like structure. Dad once again told me about 'Joe Pachoe' the man that was lost in the wilderness. Dad maintained that it was more than a story but he really didn't have any proof of his existence. He heard about 'Joe Pachoe' when he was a kid and was led to believe that the 'Joe' story took place in these woods. I asked Dad if he knew anything more about 'Joe Pachoe'. He said it was rumored that Joe had been a lumberjack and had been hit on the head by a falling branch. He became mentally affected because of it and he could not figure how to get out of the woods.

People reported seeing this mysterious man, dressed in rags, with long hair and beard, that always ran away from them as soon as contact was made.

Dad personally had never seen Joe, but one day about 1930 he said, "My friend, Ralph and I were hunting snowshoe rabbits not far from here and we heard a sound off to our right and got a glimpse of a man moving in the underbrush. He was on the other side of the stream and we only saw him for about two or three seconds. We could not figure out if he was still standing there or if he had gone over a hill. Both Ralph and I had chills run up our backs." "Was that really Joe Pachoe?" I asked. "At that time, I didn't know if he was a dangerous person or just an old man, confused about where he was. Ralph and I spent a fair amount of time wondering how he survived because when we saw him, if it was him, it was early December and the ground was covered with snow and we already had several days of temperatures below 0° F. We thought about getting across this stream on the sluice dam timbers and looking for tracks, but both of us were too chicken to do that. Actually, we high-tailed it out of there and went home. Come to think of it, where we were hunting was just east of the meadows and not far from where you found that tangle of trees," Dad said. "Let's take your flashlight and go look. It can't be much more than a quarter of a mile from here."

Mom said, "Hold on here. I don't want to be traipsing off through the brush and I certainly don't want to sit here and wait for you two to return." Mom had a good point so it was left that I would look with my flashlight and, if need be, I could send a note to Dad and he could come and see the den in the tangle of trees.

Mom wanted to know if I had come up with an idea for a book. I told her that I had been so busy writing in my diary that maybe that would be a book. I showed her my diary and I already had over 100 pages written, which reminded me that Mom needed to buy me two more thick spiral notebooks and send them with Dad as I am near the end of the second notebook. Mom wondered if there was danger of me leaving the notebooks in camp when I leave and I told her that I put both notebooks in my food pail that is covered and hanging on a rope over a big branch above us. She agreed that that was a very good idea. She hinted that she would like to read what I had written, but I said, "Not right now. Maybe if it is good enough to be a book, but right now it is private. Sorry, Mom."

Dad said he had been doing some thinking about the sluice dam and asked a couple of old timers about any memory they might have of the dam. These are two guys that work on the railroad and have lived around Spooner all their lives. Neither one actually saw the dam because they were young boys when the dam apparently was built in the late 1890s. One of the men, Fred, said his dad worked for a logging crew that logged the woods about two miles east of the dam. Fred's dad knew of the dam and he knew some of the loggers. He said they had a camp up on the big hill to the east of the dam. He said that camp had a crew of 30 and the 'bull of the woods' was Hans Larson. The camp had a cook shack, with an eating area, a bunkhouse and a blacksmith shop. Fred thought the remnants of the old camp might still be visible. He guessed that the pine logs were cut and the teamsters used horses, or oxen, to pull them near the stream downstream from the dam. Crews piled the logs on the bank ready to be rolled into the flood when the dam was opened. Fred and his dad found the old camp once about 1924, or so. By then all that was left were a few rafters, some shingles and small logs. The logs used to build the buildings were hauled away to make lumber. They could see remains of all three buildings. As Fred remembers the location, the camp was northeast of the pond with the beaver dam on it. It was up on the big hill and about three-quarters of a mile from the pond.

Dad said he had some vacation time coming up and wanted to have me look for the old logging camp with him. He would have all of the next week off and other than going to visit Duluth one day, Mom and Dad planned to go fishing a couple days, but maybe he could come to my camp and we go looking for the old logging camp. I asked Dad if he could go to the library and check out a book or two about logging in this area. He said he would and he would bring the books with him when he came to look for the camp.

Since he would not be driving the train on Friday, I asked Dad and Mom to get a bag ready for me and Dad could bring it with him. I said any day this week will be OK, but later in the week might be better so we can keep on the schedule of keeping me supplied. That idea was fine with both of them.

Mom and Dad decide it is time to head for home and Dad said tentatively he would plan to come on Thursday. He wanted to look at the tangle of trees so he would bring a flashlight, also. He had a very strong magnet that he would bring along. He thought that if we did find the site of the old logging camp we could use the magnet to see if we could find any iron or steel from old horse shoes, chains, nails and other things that might get attracted to the magnet. I hope Mom can call Margaret Burns to see if she is feeling better.

## June 22, 1948 - Early.

It is raining this morning. No search for the logging camp today. I hear a tree frog nearby and another tree frog answers from somewhere across the stream. Tonight is build a fire night to sterilize the water and I will try to catch enough trout for supper. Meanwhile, I am sleepy so will crawl back in my tent and sleep.

## June 22, 1948 - Late.

Rain stopped about midday and by late afternoon brush and other vegetation had dried off some. I dug some worms out of my stash and head for the northeast curve. This is a part of the 'Beaver' that curves to the left in a fairly wide sweep. There are two places where the stream undercuts the bank and I could feel two nice hiding places with my feet when I explored it earlier.

I step into the water upstream of the two targets. I float the worm into the first undercut and bang - there is a strong strike. I set the hook and fight this fish. I could see it was a beauty. It ran downstream and I ran with it. It went to the left across a rapids and swam under a log that protruded from the bank. This trout got my line snagged under the log. When I got the line unengaged, the fish was gone. It would have been at least a two pounder and I would have let it go anyway. Boy, that was exciting. Anyway, I know there is at least one nice trout in this part of the stream.

I fish the undercut, but no action. That doesn't surprise me because my fish swam through that area and very likely frightened the fish there. My splashing in the stream, as I ran after the fish, probably really scared them. Trout are very wary, any motion, sounds, shadows or vibrations put them on high alert and your chances of catching them are all but gone.

I continue downstream toward the straight hole. There are a series of rapids with several 'trout holes' in them and I had found them earlier. I float the worm into the first one and bang! A fat eight and one-half inch brook trout nails it. I pick some grass to put in my creel and put this nice trout in on the grass. I hook up another worm and over to the next trout hole which is behind a rock. I float the worm in and kapow! A trout hits it hard. I fight it briefly and go to lift it out and it falls off and back into the water. I could see it was about ten inches long.

I could see the worm was still there, but somehow the trout pushes the worm off the hook and on to the line. I am able to reset the worm and I decide to try the same hole again. Kapow! There is another very hard hit and I set the hook and partially lift the trout out of the water before the hook pulls out. It appeared to be about ten inches long and my guess is that it was the same fish. By now, the worm is pretty chewed up so I replace it with a fresh worm. I toss the old worm in the water so the current will take it to the trout hole and maybe this lucky fish will grab the worm and there will be no hook in it. I tried the same hole again and no luck. So I move downstream to a trout hole by the right side of the rapids. There is a good hard strike and I am able to catch a fat nine inch brookie. I decided that these two trout would be enough for my supper tonight. By now, the ferns are waist high, nettles are head high and other vegetation is thick and it makes walking anywhere besides the trail very difficult. Some of this vegetation leans over the stream and makes fishing near the banks more difficult than a month earlier.

By now I am on the big sweep which is where my campsite is located. I step out of the 'Beaver' and clean my two trout. As I clean the larger trout, I discover the remains of the worm I tossed into the stream. Apparently this fish was the same one that I had on my line twice, or it was a different fish that saw the worm and swam several feet to grab it and swallow it. I really admire these trout that live in this relatively small stream, living through high and low water levels, high and low water temperatures, frozen ice on most of the stream in the winter and floods that flush lots of dirt and debris into the water.

Somehow these trout manage to reproduce and continue to outsmart many fishermen like they have been doing for many, many years in this stream alone. Their extreme wariness has been of great use for their continued existence. I wonder how these trout got to the stream in the first place. I have read in a book about a mountain man, Jim Bridger. He told about catching nice brook trout in beaver ponds at 10,000 to 11,000 feet up in the mountains. I wonder how those trout got to those ponds. My guess is that they kept swimming upstream and eventually got to the place where the beaver pond was before the beaver built a dam. Anyway I looked at it, my hat was off to these brook trout that are able to live in a wide range of running water and maybe in lakes also.

Tonight, when I ate the tasty, pink meat of my two brook trout, I had the feeling that these fish must be some of the feistiest, adaptable animals on this earth. I felt it was a tribute to my skills, meager as they are, to be able to catch these wonderful hard fighting fish. I hope Dad brings another letter from Savannah when he visits Thursday.

## June 23, 1948 - Early.

The three foxes were sleeping outside my tent when I woke up. The three pups were in a pile about ten feet from my tent and when I came out of the tent they woke up, but did not run away. I moved carefully and sat on my camp stool for a few minutes. The pups fell back asleep so I got up and lowered my food bucket down and fixed a bowl of Cheerios and condensed milk. The pups smelled the food and got up and stood about four feet away. I tossed a couple Cheerios toward one pup and all three made a dive to see what I tossed. In a flash, the two Cheerios got wolfed down. I tossed several more cereal wheels to them and then held some in my hand. One pup slowly came forward and smelled my hand and then picked the Cheerios off my hand. I left my hand out and that pup came back and licked my hand. I put several Cheerios in my hand and all three came up and helped themselves. I did this three more times and then I thought I better not encourage them as I certainly didn't want them to be dependent on me. I finished eating my Cheerios and by then one pup came and sat down about a foot from my knees. I reached out to see if I could pet its head, but as I brought my hand close to its head it tried to smell my hand so I could not pet it, but it licked my hand twice. Finally, I stood up and the foxes ran off about twenty-five feet and seemed ready to go back toward the den.

I heard the owls last night and it seems like there are at least three of them and it seemed like two of the owls were in the big pines by my tent. I could hear a catbird meowing to the southeast. I can hear two tree frogs talking back and forth with their bird like songs. As I was cleaning up from breakfast, I heard a bird sound coming from the ground about two feet away. I watched and, in a few seconds, I saw a very small mouse like critter run from one patch of pine needles to another. It was the smallest critter I have ever seen. I heard that same bird song a couple of times during deer season. I will ask Dad what it is. Today I am going to take my flashlight and look in the tangle of trees which may have been a den or a place for someone to live.

## June 23, 1948 - Late.

WOW! What a day. I took my flashlight and gun and went to the tangle. As I walked on the west edge of the meadows I nearly stepped on a duck and her babies. The duck flew off squawking like crazy and the twelve to fifteen baby ducks scattered from the nest and hid in the tall grass of the meadow. I backed away about 75 feet and sat down behind a bush. It wasn't long and the mother duck came flying down and landed about where the nest was. She made some purring sounds which apparently the baby ducks recognized and they came back to the nest. These babies appear to have just been hatched because they were very small.

I think the mother will lead them to the stream which is about 100 yards away. They will catch insects to survive and once in the water they will eat algae, insects and other weeds. The mother duck looked like a mallard so these babies will learn to 'puddle' which means they pick things off the bottom to eat, but don't dive for them. I read that in my science class book. Dad said that lots of baby ducks get eaten by fish. I wonder if that includes trout. I guess the trout would be fairly large, like 14-15 inches at least to be able to swallow a baby duck. As they get older and larger they are probably less apt to get eaten by trout in Beaver Brook.

I continued on to the tangle and made my way into the opening. I turned on the flashlight and looked around. Someone had shoved lots of branches together to make a ceiling in this shelter. Grass and mud had been packed into the ceiling sticks so it appeared to be able to shed water. The shelter ran back under a large spruce tree that had blown over, pointed toward the west. The opening I came in opened to the southeast and actually a big tip up of roots blocked the entrance, but I could still walk in.

The space inside was long and narrow. About twenty feet long and eight to nine feet wide. More branches had been pushed into existing branches to form a wall. Mud and grass had been added to the branches to make a snug wall. Some of the grass and mud had fallen out, but I could see that it had been there. On the east end of this space I could see evidence of a fire. There was a small pit and bits of charred wood remained in the pit. Near the pit was an area that had been dug out and was about six feet long and about one foot deep. There was remnants of grass in this dug out depression. It appeared to be a sleeping area. There were no other dug out areas but it appeared that the entire space in this shelter had been reinforced with branches and plastered with a mixture of grass and mud. Someone definitely spent a fair amount of time in this shelter. I wondered if someone had died there, but I saw no evidence of that.

I shined my light on all parts of the shelter, including the ceiling. My light showed a strange piece of wood stuck in the branches of the ceiling. I moved closer and looked at it. It appeared to be a part of a branch that was carved flat on one side. It looked like it was about two feet long or at least that much was visible. I reached up and pulled this piece of wood out of the ceiling. There appeared to be letters carved into the flat side. I took this piece outside to see if I would make out what the letters said.

The piece of wood was very old and had several small holes in it made by powder post beetles as well as other beetles. I brushed off some cobwebs and finally I could read the letters. JOE PACHOE, Dec. 1929 - Mar. 1930. How about that? Could this have been home sweet home for Joe Pachoe for part of a winter? Did this guy really exist or was that carved stick done by someone else?

I held it and looked at it. If this was done by the real Joe Pachoe then he must have spent part of the 1929-30 winter here. How could he possibly keep warm enough? What did he eat? Maybe he had a gun and could shoot a deer, rabbits, partridge, etc. If he didn't have a gun, perhaps he could snare rabbits or partridge. Maybe he found grubs in dead trees and used them to catch trout in the stream, if he had hooks and line to catch fish.

Someone, maybe Joe Pachoe, apparently lived in this shelter one winter about 20 years ago. This entire shelter thing could be a hoax. If it is, then someone put a great effort into reinforcing with branches and putting grass and mud on the walls and ceiling.

I put the carved, flattened stick back in the ceiling where I found it. I stepped back outside and looked around. This shelter was on the southwest side of the meadows which is an open area of three or four acres with almost no trees growing there. I wondered if that was a field as part of a farm at one time. That is a very real possibility. The land is flat and appeared to be quite productive. Dad said that, back at the turn of the century, about 1900, nearly all of Washburn County was privately owned. During the depression, many people could not pay their taxes and the land reverted back to the county. This property is owned by the State of Wisconsin but they may have bought it from the county after it was taken over for non-payment of taxes. I searched the edge of the opening looking for any sign that it may have been plowed at one time.

I walked around the edge of the opening and did not find any evidence that it ever was a field. Next, I searched for any evidence of any buildings or evidence of a building site. After about three hours of searching, I concluded that the meadows must be a natural meadow of three or four acres that just grows grass and a few small shrubs, but trees don't grow there. It seems strange to me, but Dad said the meadows were there when he was a kid and he could not see much of a change in his lifetime.

I decided to explore and observe some of the holes as the stream ran on the east side of the meadows. By now the stream was two or three times larger than by the bridge. Several springs and streams have fed into the 'Beaver' by now.

I go to the northeast part of the meadows and find a nice deep left hand curve that goes a short distance and then drops into a deep hole at least four and one-half to five feet deep. I knelt down by the west side of the hole and watched. I kept looking for about thirty minutes and in that time I saw one nice fish about sixteen inches long. I am pretty sure it was a trout. Towards the end of my watching, I took an alder leaf, rolled it into a small ball and flicked it out into the current. It only went about three feet when, all at once, there was a huge roll as some very large fish came up and grabbed the crumpled up leaf. That fish was in the four pound class. Apparently it didn't like the leaf because in a few seconds, the leaf floated back to the surface. When the water is high, I will come to this hole, which I named the north meadows hole, and try to catch that big trout. The hole was large and I would have a decent chance to land this beauty. I just need to wait for high water. By now it was late afternoon, so I followed the stream along the edge of the meadow and came to a nice undercut where the stream runs under the overhanging bank. There were no overhanging branches in the way so this looked like a great hole also. When I got back to camp, I realized that I had not packed a sandwich for lunch and I was hungry, so I had a early supper of a can of Spam and an orange.

**June 24, 1948 - Early.**

I was lying in the tent when I heard something splashing in the stream only about 100 feet away. I grab my gun and poke my head out of the tent. I can't see anything so I crawl out of the tent and stand up. Then I could see it. It was a large black bear!! It was walking in the rapids and it made quite a commotion. The bear continued down stream for fifty feet or so.  It decided to leave the stream and go east, away from my camp.

WOW!  That was the first wild bear I had ever seen.  I knew that there were a few around because each year during deer season, hunters will shoot a few bear and some get their picture in the paper.  This changes my outlook around camp.  I did not think there were any bear around camp.  My little .22 caliber rifle would not be much of a weapon if this bruin decided to attack.  I am glad that I wash cans out and splash the rinse water over a wide area.  The can is added to the bag with the others and pulled up in the branches of a tree about a hundred yards from camp, but along the trail I walk when I go to meet Dad's train.  That Spam can probably would really attract bear, foxes, raccoons and others, if I didn't wash it out good and put it in the bag and pull it up into the tree.

## June 24, 1948  - Late.

I followed the little stream under the trestle.  Boy that is beautiful east of the trestle.  The big trees and the small stream disappearing under the roots for many feet and then reappearing.  It is a wonderful place to visit.  I do see small trout in some of the pools.  I continue under the trestle and follow the stream to the marsh where the shy poke was pumping water when Elon Casey and I saw her on her nest.  I am curious if there are babies in the nest.  I know that I am in a pasture with cows and since I really don't know much about their behavior, I am cautious as I approach the marsh where we saw the shy poke.

I get to where I think she is and I look for several minutes and then - there she is with her beak straight up in the air.

I don't see any cows so I take off my shoes and socks and slowly wade into the marsh to see what is in the nest. I got to about three feet away and the shy poke has not moved a muscle. I just stood there for at least five minutes and finally the mother shy poke slowly stepped off the nest and I could see two little fluff balls that were sitting in the nest made of grass and reeds and holding their beaks up in the air, but their beaks were closed. The mother shy poke had only gone about five feet from the nest and was standing, watching me. I quietly talked to her and then I back tracked out of the marsh. I put my shoes and socks back on and sat there and watched mother shy poke. Finally, after about ten minutes, she slowly went back to the nest.

I decided to go back the way I came by following the small stream. I went only a short distance when, all of a sudden, I saw several cows in my intended path. Now what? I could not go to my right as the marsh was there. I really didn't have much choice. I was a little lucky, in that the cows had not seen me. That would not be a good thing to be chased by cows in an unfamiliar pasture.

I circled to my left and there was enough brush that the cows didn't see me. I had gone about one hundred yards and thought I had gotten around the cows when, all of a sudden, I walked around some brush and there were seven more - right in my intended path. Now what? These cows had seen me, but they were not coming after me either. I stepped back behind the bushes I was near and circled to my left some more. I had gone about a hundred yards when I could hear some heavy feet running in my direction. I started running to the north hoping that the fence I thought was there would come into view - soon!

I looked over my shoulder and saw six or eight brown, brown and white and black and white cows kicking up their heels, but they were running at least as fast as I was. I did have about a fifty yard lead, but I didn't know how far away the fence was. I ran as fast as I could and finally I see the fence. I got to the fence and rolled under and stepped back. I watched the cows come running up. The rest of the herd apparently wanted to get into the action as they came running up also. All together there were seventeen cows. They just stood on the other side of the fence and they actually looked friendly, so I moved close to the fence and held my hand out. Two cows walked right up and smelled my hand - one gave my hand a lick. Boy, it felt like very coarse sand paper.

I talked to these cows and they all seemed friendly. I figured out that they were just curious and didn't intend to harm me. I wondered where the barn was that these cows go to get milked. I remember seeing cows walking under the highway south of Spooner and it could have been these cows. Apparently there is an underpass so cattle can go from pastures on one side to pastures on the other side of the highway.

The cows started grazing so I crawled back under the fence and walked near a cow, but close to the fence. She didn't pay any attention to me. I walked up to another one and had the same result. Finally, I realized that they were just curious and when I ran they thought my behavior was strange so they ran after me.

By the time I ran where I did to escape these cows, I was part way up the big hill that the Hilltop Cabins were on. I could already get a little view of the Beaver Brook valley and I wanted to see more. I went higher and I could see the buildings of the farm on the hill. Finally, I stopped about fifty yards from the barn and looked out over the big woods across the railroad tracks. What a sight. The valley that Beaver Brook ran in was evident. In the background to the east was the high hill which must have been more than a mile long. The giant white pines rose twenty to thirty feet above the other trees. Way to the left, or toward the north, the terrain flattens out more. Towards the right, or south, there were more big hills and many, many huge white pines. I could see the marsh where the shy poke was and the open field between the marsh and the railroad tracks. About then I heard a steam engine signal for a crossing to my south. I guessed it was the crossings at the cranberry marsh. In about two or three minutes here comes the train. It was a passenger train being pulled by one of the last steam engines that are still being used. That was a beautiful sight as the old steamer rolled along at a good clip, putting out smoke and steam, pulling twelve cars with passengers and mail.

By now, it was late afternoon and I was about to head back to camp when I saw a girl come out of the barn and walk toward the northeast. After awhile, she apparently called to the cows and it sounded like, "Come boss, come boss." I ducked back into the woods and watched this girl round up about fifteen cows and herd them up the hill to the barn. The cows all went in the barn and the girl closed the door. I guess it was time to get milked and it was time for me to hightail it to my camp. Tonight was a fire building night, so I will try to catch enough trout for supper. I wonder where the bear is? I dig some worms and decided to try the hole just upstream from the sluice dam. I caught three trout, all were about eight inches long.  I started the fire to fry the trout and sterilize the water.  All is good tonight.

**June 25, 1948 - Early**.

Dad comes today,  I hope.  I heard the owls during the night.  Tree frogs were singing this morning.  The three fox pups came running from the south.  I tossed some Cheerios toward them and they pounced on them and looked for more.  These pups have gotten noticeably bigger since I first saw them in early June.  I can hear a long howl off in the distance.  Is that a wolf?  Whatever it is, I am glad it is quite far away - at least for now.

**June 25, 1948 - Late**.

Dad did arrive by early morning.  He has a thermos bottle of coffee and another one for cocoa.  We sit and drink our drinks and talk.  Dad and Mom really are thoughtful, kind hearted people.  He told me that Mom called Margaret Burns and she is getting along pretty good.  Dad also produced a letter from Savannah.  I will read that later.

I told Dad about what I think is Joe Pachoe's shelter.  He wants to look at it before we search for the old logging camp.  Dad and Mom fished on Tuesday and Wednesday and went to Cable Lake and Shell Lake.  They had great luck and caught their limit of pan fish both days.  Dad was really excited about possibly finding Joe Pachoe's shelter. We drank up and grabbed our flashlights and Dad had the powerful magnet.  We headed to the meadows and Joe's shelter.

When  we arrived at the shelter, Dad wanted to go in first,

and he did. He was astounded when he looked around. He was impressed with the extra branches being worked into the existing branches. The mixtures of mud and grass being applied to the branches to form the walls and ceiling really impressed him. The fire pit and the apparent bed near the fire pit really seemed to make Dad stop and ponder. I wondered why.

I pointed out the half-carved stick with letters and numbers on it and he took it down and went outside with it. He studied the letters and numbers and concluded that it said, JOE PACHOE Dec. 1929 - Mar. 1930. I told him that I agreed with that. Dad said, "The guy my pal and I saw must have been Joe. It was the winter of 1929-30. Imagine that. Apparently the story about Joe Pachoe might be true and he must have spent the winter right here. If he had a gun and shells he could shoot a deer or rabbits or partridge. What happens if he runs out of shells? If he went to get more shells, why wouldn't he stay in town, or at least in a house? Maybe being hit by that tree limb really messed up his mind."

I could tell that finding this shelter really hit Dad hard. Maybe the fact that it might have been a made up story and maybe seeing the mysterious person while rabbit hunting 18 years ago, is causing Dad some anxiety. He put the carved stick back in the ceiling and we went to the sluice dam timbers and crossed the 'Beaver' and headed to where we thought the old logging camp might be.

Since the trappers cabin was on the way to the logging camp, I showed Dad the cabin under the downed tree. We crowded in and Dad looked around. I told him that apparently Frank Steffan owned this but lost it in 1934 because he could not pay his taxes. Dad said, "I knew Frank. He worked on the railroad but he got killed during a snowstorm in 1934. A train hit the hand car he was on and killed Frank and one other man." That explains why many things still remain in the cabin.

We went northeast from the beaver pond and got up on the big hill. First we just looked for any tell tale signs maybe the builders had to do a little digging to get the buildings level. We searched for about two hours and then took a lunch break. As we sat on a downed tree, we tried to think where we would build three good sized buildings for a logging camp. I said, "It should be level." Dad said, "It should not be near the edge of the hill. The road leading to it should not go up any big hills. Maybe we should look for any sign of a road and that may lead us to the building site."

We moved further north on top of the big hill. Then we saw it. Some ruts in the ground that seemed to come from the northeast. We turned around and tried to follow the ruts, but they disappeared from time to time. We could see the general direction they were heading so we carefully followed and if we lost the trail, one of us stopped and stood where we last saw evidence of the trail. We continued for at least one-half mile and then the tracks seemed to end. We looked around and saw one place where it looked like dirt might have been shoveled away to provide a level spot for a corner of a building. Dad took the magnet out of his shoulder pouch and started sweeping near what looked like a spot for a corner of a building. Maybe there are nails there, or nearby.

Dad swept with the magnet, but didn't find any steel or

iron.  We scratched away the leaves and he swept some more and bingo!  All at once, he had a big nail stuck to his magnet.  Maybe this is the place, but maybe it is some hunting camp also.  We kept scraping the leaves away and sweeping with the magnet.  More nails, some were small like roofing nails.

After two hours, we found the outline of one building. We broke off branches and pushed them  into the ground at the corners.  This building was about forty feet long and sixteen feet wide.  Too big for a hunting camp - maybe. We only had an hour left before Dad had to head back. We decided to look for scrap heaps of old horseshoes, broken chain links, oxen shoes and possible a dump where the cook, or bull cook, pitched tin cans that certain foods came in.

Dad stood looking at the outline of the building we found. "Could this be the blacksmith shop?" he asked.  "If so there should be some iron around somewhere."  We wondered where the doors might have been in this building.  Dad said he had seen pictures of logging camps and some buildings had a double door near the middle of one of the sidewalls.  We decided to search with the magnet where we thought the doorway might have been. Perhaps the blacksmith pitched broken parts on to a heap near the door.

After about twenty minutes of scratching around and using the magnet, Dad found an oxen shoe stuck to the magnet.  We looked closely at it and found part of it was broken off.  Dad said, "This must be the place."  We proceeded to scratch and sweep with the magnet and found a broken horseshoe, a part of a log chain and several non-descript bits of iron.   By this time we were sure we had found a logging camp, but Dad needed to get back, so we headed for the sluice dam timbers so we could cross the 'Beaver'.  We got to camp and Dad picked up the two thermos and my bag of laundry and cans.  Dad said this was a very good day finding where Joe Pachoe may have wintered and finding partial remains of the logging camp and doing it with his son was special.  He gave me a hug and then headed out.  It was a special day. I wonder if there are many fourteen year old boys as lucky as I am.  I have a wonderful, loving Mom and Dad.  I live in a great country, the USA,  and I can camp out and spend the summer in this beautiful public forest on the banks of a beautiful trout stream.   Besides, I have met a wonderful, good looking trout fisherman, or fisherwoman, who just sent me a letter that I will open and read now.

Before I open it, I see the SWAK on the back of the envelope.  I don't have any idea and I don't want to ask my mom and dad.   I will just have to wait and ask Savannah.   Darn, I should have written a letter to Savannah and given to  Dad.  Maybe it would not get to her before they left to come home.  Anyway, Savannah was really enjoying visiting all the monuments in Washington, D. C.   She was really impressed by Arlington National Cemetery.  The White House visit was outstanding as was a visit to the Capitol.  She will be on her way home by the time I read this.  She is really anxious to meet me by the big pine on Thursday, July 2$^{nd}$. I am really anxious to see Savannah, but she wrote something at the end of her letter that I wonder about. OVELA.  That girl is full of all kinds of surprises and she sure has gotten my attention.

I asked Dad about the little mouse like critter that sounds like a bird as it runs around under the leaves. He said it more than likely is a shrew. They have teeth like a dog and live on grubs, worms and insects and apparently will attack and kill a much bigger mouse. He has seen and heard them during deer season before much snow has fallen. Spam was the main menu item tonight.

## June 26, 1948 - Early.

During the night I could hear a slurping sound coming from the stream. It was fully dark but there was a quarter moon quite low in the western sky. I took my flashlight and went to the stream. The slurping continued and finally I got something in my light beam. It was a trout catching some kind of insect that was on the surface! Actually, there were apparently several trout feasting on these bugs on a fairly quiet part of the stream.

I watched for about fifteen minutes and was impressed by how many trout were eating bugs. I have heard of trout fishermen using dry flies at dusk, but not in the dark of the night. It looks like if a person knew what fly to use and could see it, the trout would probably grab the fly. That kind of fishing does not appeal to me.

The fox pups made a run through camp but did not stay. They were in a roughhouse mood. Heard lots of frogs last night - seemed to be coming from a small swamp southeast of camp. Actually, it was part of Beaver Brook at one time and that part of the stream was a big meander and, during high water, the stream decided to go straight and not meander. So that part of the stream got cut off and became a swampy area. I wonder what happened to the trout?

I am fascinated by the cows I saw yesterday and have made up my mind to search them out and not run from them. I think they will be friendly toward me.

## June 16, 1948 - Late.

I crossed under the trestle and crawled under the fence. I headed toward the shy poke swamp, and as I was nearly there, I heard a vehicle coming so I ducked behind some bushes. Pretty soon a car came into view on the trail by the edge of the marsh. There was a man driving the car, a woman riding in the front seat and a young boy in the back seat. The trunk was propped open and I could see handles of some kind of tools sticking out. The car passed about 75 feet from me and continued along the trail, drove into the small stream at a crossing and continued to the large open field. They drove up to the fence by the railroad tracks and stopped there. All three got out of the car and took the tools and started doing something with the fence.

I decided to look for the cows to the west of where I was. If they weren't there I would try to find them another day. I crawled backward and got behind enough brush  so I would not be seen by the fence workers. I stood up and began walking west and in about one hundred yards I found several cows, munching on the  grass about one hundred fifty feet from me. I spoke to them and they looked up at me but did not come after me. I continued walking toward them and talking to them. Amazingly, the cows went back to their grazing. I continued walking toward them and got right up to the first two and they did not pay any attention to me at all. I walked between two cows and got near the rest of this small group and none of the cows paid any attention to me. Several cows had horns, but not all of them.

I was reminded about a poem that our fifth grade teacher, Mrs. Robinson, read to us about the cow. All I can remember was the cows had two hookers, two lookers, a swishy swashy, four down hangers and a big long tongue. Looking at the cows near me, I could see curved horns (hookers), two eyes (lookers), a  tail ( the swishy swashy) and four milk handles (four down hangers).

I left the cows and headed toward the big hill with the farm on it. I was so impressed by the view over the wildlife area, I wanted to see it again. I carefully made my way to the spot I was before when I saw this beautiful view. I did not see or hear anyone, so I took in this beautiful sight. The big hill to the east as a backdrop was impressive as were the huge white pines toward the south. That was a beautiful sight! The railroad tracks and the trestle formed the lower limit of my view. If I had any art skills, I would try to capture this view, but  I will have to settle for a memory.

I decide to head back to camp, so I skirt around the field in front of me, cross under the trestle and return to camp. Tonight is fire night so I will dig some worms and try to catch enough trout for supper. I decided to try the north meadow hole. This hole is a fair distance from camp so I took my pole, creel, landing net and worms and started walking with my hip boots on.

I got to the hole and eased into the water which was nearly

to the top of my hip boots. I floated a worm near the left side of the hole. I got a strong hit and set the hook on a nice ten inch brookie. I wanted to net this fish more for practice than anything else. I grabbed the landing net which was for netting lake fish because it was bigger than the kind of net trout fishermen carry around their shoulder. I maneuvered the trout and reached out with the net, but found that my arm with the fly rod was in was fully extended while my arm with the net was also fully extended. The problem was that I still could not reach the trout. I tried shortening up my grip on the fly rod and now I could get the trout into the net. I pulled some grass for the creel and put this nice trout in with the grass.

I baited the hook and floated it on the right side of the hole and nothing happened. I pulled the line in and put one split shot on the leader to get the worm deeper in the water. The worm got floated and I let out more line and then I could feel a fish on the line so I set the hook and felt a heavy fish. It came to life and made a run to the left side of the pool. It felt very powerful. This pool appeared to be free of branches and other obstructions. The fish moved back to the right and I tried to turn it toward me but could not do it. The fish turned away from me and ran to the back of the hole. I tried to hold it and I was able to keep it from leaving the hole. It did take out lots of line, so I began pulling the line back onto the reel. The fish made a run right at me so, all at once, I had lots of slack line to reel in. The fish stopped about eight feet directly in front of me and when I got the slack line reeled in, I tried to get it to move, but it would not have any of that. Finally, I tried more force and that made the big fish move hard to the right and when I tried to hold it, the hook pulled out and came flying right at me. WOW! That was a three or four pounder. I didn't even feel bad that this beauty got away. I would have released it after I measured it, anyway. Besides, I know it is still in this hole and maybe Savannah can catch it using flies. Boy, having that big trout on my line was exciting. It is the largest trout I have ever had on my line.

I still needed to catch one more trout so I went back upstream to the meadow curve hole and was able to catch an eight and one-half inch brookie. I clean the two trout and head for camp. As I came into camp, I saw a very small owl sitting on one of the white pines branches of a big tree near my tent. It was only about six feet off the ground and wasn't over six inches tall. I stopped when I saw it and I was about twenty feet from it. I watched this very interesting owl as it looked at me with nearly half closed eyes. From time to time, it turned its head and

Saw-Whet Owl

looked around. I watched for about twenty minutes and then slowly moved closer. In a few minutes, I had moved to within five feet of the little owl. Nothing changed - it just looked at me. I didn't have any idea what kind of owl it was. I hope Mom or Dad will know.

I decided not to scare the owl if I could help it. I built the fire and started frying the trout. I was busy doing that and didn't look at the owl for a few minutes. Then I looked at it and saw that it had moved to a little different spot on the limb, but now it had a dead mouse under one of its claws. Apparently, the little owl spotted a mouse and grabbed it. I expect that the owl will eat the mouse.

The big trout is on my mind. It must live in that north meadow hole, or nearby. I wonder if it is the biggest trout in that hole. I had never thought of trout, or any other fish, as anything other than an animal I wanted to catch. Did it have a family? Do fish have a mom and dad that looks after them? Apparently I have had the idea that fish are somehow not able to show love, or emotion, like we can. Maybe that is wrong. Anyway, I am glad the big trout got away today. What is wrong with that idea? What am I doing trying to catch this big trout? Will it make me feel better because I caught it? Is the act of trying to catch a big trout what it is really all about? I do enjoy fishing and trying to outsmart the trout, or other fish. I also enjoy eating fish, especially trout. I seem to have a problem deciding if catching fish is OK or should I not do it, or attempt to do it. I need to do some more thinking about this and maybe talk to Mom and Dad about it. Maybe Savannah could help me understand my uncertainty about catching fish.

## June 27, 1948 - Early.

The little owl is gone. That little bird was one of the most interesting birds I have ever seen. I hope it will come back. Since today is Saturday, I think I will stay around camp as I need to get more fire wood put under the tarp. I found several dead trees about 150 yards from camp. I begin cutting them up with the Swede saw and hauling the wood to camp. On about the fourth trip, I looked at the lower limbs of the pine trees by the tent and there was the little owl. About two feet away was another little owl. Both were watching me with half open eyes. I sat down and watched these two owls. The one owl watched me, but would swivel its head while it looked around from time to time. The other owl, which looked slightly different from the other owl, watched me and looked around too, but once it looked up in the big pine tree it was in. I looked up and watched because that owl did more than glace up. About twenty feet above the two owls, there are three really small owls sitting on a limb. Ah ha, these two must be mom and dad and the three little ones are the kids. Maybe they have been up in this big pine tree ever since I got here three and one-half weeks ago. I hope Mom and Dad can see them when they visit next time. I need a haircut.

## June 27, 1948 - Late.

As I worked with the wood, I could hear a machine of some kind running west of me and west of the tracks. Curiosity got the best of me, plus I was getting tired of hauling the firewood to camp. I decided to investigate the machine sound so I went up my trail to the tracks. I just stepped out of the woods within about twenty-five feet from the railroad tracks. I started walking again when, all at once, someone said, "Hello!" I looked to my right and here sat a man, sitting on a duffel bag, or knapsack. I said, "Hello," and turned to go back down my trail toward camp. The man said, "Where are you going so fast? I won't hurt you." He sounded friendly so I stopped to at least visit with this man. I did notice a crutch laying on the ground near him. He said, "My name is Earl. Earl Burke, and I am on my way to Spooner." I asked him, "What is the crutch for?" He said, "I was in the war and got my leg shot up on Iwo Jima. That was a little over three and one-half years ago and it has not healed properly and became infected from the original injury." I asked him, "Do you have any family in Spooner?" He said, "No, I grew up in Superior and went to school and graduated from Superior Central High School. I continued on to college at Superior State Teachers College. I had completed one year there when my buddy and I decided to join up with the Marines. We took our basic training at a camp at Parris Island, South Carolina. We trained very hard and felt we were a strong fighting force. We worked together as teamwork was very important for our performance to be at a high level. We landed on Iwo Jima and really took heavy losses."

He said, "I had hopped the train at Eau Claire and was headed for Spooner. The train stopped by some large buildings and I got off because I thought it was Spooner. It turned out to be the cranberry marsh and the train dropped off a box car loaded with barrels. There were too many people around and I could not hop back on the train as it pulled out. I wandered up a road and came to a shack with a young Indian couple living there. They invited me in for something to eat. They sure were very nice and I ended up staying with them for two days. They tried to find someone that could take me to Spooner, but had no luck. I guess they thought I was a hobo, so I decided to walk the track to Spooner. This is as far as I got today. I am tired out and figured I would put my tent up and spend the night here. Things have not been going very good for me. I can't get over seeing so many of my friends killed or wounded. I can't seem to focus on things. I am a mess. I wanted to try things at Spooner because when I went back to Superior, things really fell apart. I have a brother there, but my mom and dad have both died."

I could see that this man was really down. I told him about my camp and if he wanted to put his tent under the tarp he could stay overnight. I told him I could catch trout and we could eat that tonight. He perked up when I said trout.

I helped him up and I took his duffel bag. He was able to hobble along at a pretty good clip. We reached camp and he was excited. He really liked the layout under the huge pine trees and on the bank of a beautiful stream.

I told him that I was camping all summer and didn't want any of my friends to find me and this camp. I asked him to not tell anyone about it when he got to Spooner. He said, "I will not breath a word." I asked what his name was because I could not remember it. He told me, "Earl Burke." I told him my name and he reached out and shook my hand - hard - and told me, "Good to meet you."

We looked for the best place for Earl to pitch his tent and decided on a spot just under the tarp. I dug some worms, took my fly rod and creel, put on my hip boots and headed for the steep bank hole upstream. I reached the upstream side of this hole with its buried log about a foot under water. By using my feet several days ago, I found that there was an undercut below the bank and right beside the log. It was about three feet long and really looked like a great trout spot. I put one split shot on to get the worm down into this undercut. I floated the worm and wham! Something really smacked it! I could hold the fish but I could not budge it. Finally, it moved but I could not get it out from under the overhang. After about forty seconds, I finally got the fish to the surface. I backed up and was able to guide the fish onto a gravel bar where I could grab it. Wow! It was a brown trout that was fourteen and one-half inches long. It was a beautiful fish. If I didn't have Earl to feed tonight I would have put this big guy back, but tonight it goes in the creel with the fresh grass.

This hole is finished for now so I move downstream to the northeast curve hole. This was a hole where the stream undercut the bank and then flowed to the left. There was a deep hole on the right side caused by water reflecting off the bank and then having to move left. This hole appeared to be about four feet deep according to my probing with a stick several days ago. I put a fresh worm on and began floating the worm far upstream so the worm could get to the bottom of the deep hole. It took several seconds to play the fly line out and guide the worm to the right spot.

Several seconds passed and I did not feel anything on the line. I began taking up line and, all at once, I felt a gentle tap on the line. Ah ha, a fish was after the worm. I took up a little more line and felt a gentle tap again. I set the hook and felt a good fish on the other end. It immediately came shooting out of the water and shook its head like mad. Wow! What a sight. It tried to run under the bank right in front of me, but I was able to hold it. It jumped again and I was able to move it toward me. I began backing up and was able to guide it on to a sand bar where I could grab it. It also was a brown trout thirteen inches long. Another beautiful fish. It joined the fourteen and one-half inch trout in my creel. I took my fly rod apart and headed for camp. Earl and I should both have a nice feast tonight. What the heck does OVELA mean? What language is that? Could it be Italian? That Savannah seems to be on my mind - nearly always. Anyway, it is only four more days until we meet at the big pine.

I got back near the camp and found Earl sitting on a camp stool, smoking. I had not figured on that. I certainly didn't want cigarette smoke giving away my campsite to anyone like a trout fisherman passing nearby the camp. I decide to confront Earl about this issue.

I get to camp and get a fire started and then ask Earl about his smoking in camp. I told him that he already knew I wanted to keep the campsite a secret. He said, "I know that and I realize I should not have done it in camp." I said, "I don't care if you smoke, that is your business." There was a long silence and Earl said, "You have been very friendly and kind to me. I don't want that to change, but my smoking is about the only thing I can do to help me get over some of my bad memories of the war and my buddies." There was a long pause and I was almost ready to give in when Earl said, "How would it be if I want to smoke, I walk up to the railroad tracks and smoke?" I was really relieved to hear that and said, "Earl, if you will do that, you can stay in my camp. Let's not set a time limit, but feel free to hang out here, and I am very willing to listen to anything you want to tell me. I want you to get over whatever is causing you to not do well. I will do whatever I can to help. I really admire what you and all our other servicemen and women did to win that war. Our country owes you and all who served the opportunity to get healed up and get on with your lives. I heard my mom and dad talking about the GI bill. Do you know what that is?" Earl said, "I have heard of it, but really haven't had the desire to check it out."

The two trout got fried and I boiled water. Earl really enjoyed eating the trout and he ate all of the largest one. He asked if the water was hot and I said it was. "Want a cup of coffee?" he asked. "No thanks," I said, "but go ahead." He dug in his duffel bag and got out a cup and a pouch with coffee in it. He put some of the coffee in his cup and took a ladle and filled his cup from the kettle of boiling water. He stirred his coffee and then tasted it. I could tell he really enjoyed that coffee. I dug out some of Mom's cookies and offered them to Earl. I could see Earls' hand shake as he reached for a cookie. He finished his coffee and by now it was dark. He said he was going to turn in, but before he did he said, "Nick, you are one of the kindest people I have ever met. Stay that way. Good night." Wow! I am just a kid!

### June 28, 1948  - Early.

Heard Earl shouting in the night. Could only understand a few words. One was Miller, Captain Miller. The other word was Japs. I could hear him thrashing inside his tent. I got up and got the Cheerio's and condensed milk ready for breakfast. Earl crawled out of his tent and looked around. He pointed behind me and said, "That little owl just flew up and landed on the branch." I turned and looked and sure enough, the little owl was back and it had a mouse in one of its claws. Earl said, "The owl is a saw-whet owl." I said, "There is another one, plus three babies up in this tree." We looked up in the branches about twenty feet and there sat the other adult and the three babies. Earl said, "We could walk right up to the one on the lower branch. These owls are not afraid of people and many times people can actually touch them." I asked Earl, "How do you know that?" He said, "I majored in biology at Superior State College and I studied about lots of different plants and animals." He also said, "If we watch the adult with the mouse, it will eat the mouse and then regurgitate the pieces to feed the babies."

We ate breakfast and Earl encouraged me to slowly walk up near the owl. I did and it watched me with its half opened eyes, turning its head to look around from time to time. I walked up and slowly put my hand on the branch about six inches from the owl. It watched my hand, but did not fly away.

After eating, Earl said he was going to walk up near the tracks and have a cigarette. I did some writing and kept watching the owl. Pretty soon it began tearing at the mouse with its beak. It tore the mouse into small bits and swallowed them. About the time Earl got back to camp, the owl had eaten the entire mouse. It then flew up to the branch that the three babies were on. This owl moved from baby bird to baby bird. It opened its mouth and the baby nearest it reached inside with its beak and got a morsel of the mouse. It repeated this for the other two babies and then started in again. In a few minutes  the feeding was apparently finished.

**June 28, 1948 - Late**.

Earl asked about the trout fishing. He said he had fished on the Brule River several times and caught several steelheads that weighed three to seven pounds. He had never fished on a small stream like the one by camp. He said he used spawn to catch the steelheads but he thought they might bite on worms also. Earl wanted to know what I did all day. I told him what had gone on so far. He was really intrigued by the possible discovery of Joe Pachoe's winter quarters. He asked if I could take him to it. I said I could if he thought he was up to it. I told him it is less than half mile away. He wanted to go this morning, so I took my flashlight and we set off.

Earl used his crutch some, but could walk without it some of the time. We went on the west edge of the meadows and arrived at the tangle that Joe called home. With the flashlight on, we went inside the tangle. Earl was impressed. I showed him the branch with the carving of letters and numbers. He was fascinated by the way Joe had used mud and grass to seal up the walls and ceiling.

We finally stepped out of the shelter and Earl said he heard about a guy that was lost in the wilderness for many years. He didn't know where it took place so maybe that was this Joe.

We left the tangle and headed for the four timbers of the sluice dam. Earl was really impressed with these timbers and he could picture some sort of dam built to hold back water from spring runoff to make a flood that would carry the logs down to a mill.

We stood and looked at these four timbers for a very long time without saying anything. Finally he said that his grandfather Burke had been a logger for many years. He didn't know where he did the logging and wondered if he might have done it here. Finally, we headed back to camp and got there by mid-afternoon. Earl was tired out and immediately sat on one of the camp stools. I made some peanut butter sandwiches and we ate them. I think Earl wanted to see the site of the old logging camp, but for now he was content to stay in camp. He said his leg felt pretty good, maybe walking in the woods was good for it. I wanted to find out more about his war experiences, but I would not ask him. Maybe he will volunteer sometime.

With Earl in camp, I decided to see if I could catch enough trout for supper. I am really amazed at my luck fishing, so far. I dug some worms from my stash, took my fly rod and creel, put on my hip boots and this time I took the landing net and I headed for the straight hole.

This was a long, fairly deep hole with several 'trout holes' in the rapids just above the hole. I began fishing one hundred feet above the hole and floated the worm over the first 'trout hole' in the rapids. Bang! A fat eight incher grabbed it and I landed it and put it in the creel with some fresh grass. I re-baited and moved to the next hole. No luck, on to the third. I got a good hit, but the trout got off. I tried again and this time a fat eight and one-half inch trout ended up in my creel. One more 'trout hole' produced no action so I let the worm float down into the 'straight hole'. I played out line and kept the worm on top of the water until it was in position to drop into the deep pool on the right side of the hole. Several seconds passed and I felt nothing. I started taking up line and I felt a little tap on the line. I let out a little more line and then started taking up line and I felt a little tap again. I set my feet and set the hook. I could feel a decent fish on the line. It immediately jumped out and shook like mad. It looked like about a foot long. I played it and backed up to a gravel bar where I was able to pull the trout onto the gravel. I was able to grab the trout and add it to my creel. I moved down stream to a log that protruded out into the stream. The end of the log stuck out from shore and water flowed under and around it. I floated the worm so it would go under the log and before it got there, a nine incher zipped out and grabbed it. I landed it and added it to the creel. That would be just enough for supper.

I cleaned the fish and headed for camp. Earl was not there but all his gear and tent were, so I figured he was up by the tracks smoking. I got a fire started and got a kettle of water starting to boil. Maybe Earl will want a cup of coffee before supper.

I looked up the trail and here came Earl. He got to camp just before the rain did. We hung out under the tarp and he told me he saw a black bear cross the railroad tracks going west. It was about 150 yards north of him and was just walking slowly. He said that is the first wild bear he had ever seen. Earl made a cup with coffee grounds and I went over and filled his cup with hot water. We waited for the rain to stop. It did stop after about thirty minutes. I fried the trout and we ate supper.

We sat around and talked after we finished eating. Earl said, "I really like this campsite and being in this big woods by this beautiful stream." He mostly made small talk about some of his friends from Superior and his college days. He asked about my mom and dad and I explained that I will meet Dad's train tomorrow afternoon and give him a sack with dirty clothes, empty cans and a letter about what I need by Friday's train.

It turns out that Earl played football and basketball at Superior Central High School. He played halfback on offense in football and played safety on defense. He was a guard on the basketball team. When he was a senior, the basketball team was undefeated but only played ten games as most schools cancelled athletics because of the war. He had hoped to go out for football in college but the college team was cancelled also. He was planning to try out for the team after the war but his injured leg pretty well rules that out. "Besides, I need to get my act together before I can even think of going back to college," Earl said.

As we sat there, we could hear tree frogs talking. Later on, the frogs in the small swamp started singing. It was just about dark when we started hearing owls hooting about a hundred yards away. All at once, we heard a screeching, scratchy song coming from right over our heads. Earl smiled and said, "Saw-whet owl." We turned in for the night and I could hear a howl way off in the distance.

### June 29, 1948 - Early.

I heard Earl shout and call out again last night. I recognized him saying Captain Miller. Most of what he said was mumbled. I could hear him rolling and tossing in his tent. I wondered if he may try to harm me while he was tossing and turning. He certainly must be dreaming, but he was under stress while he was dreaming. We have our Cheerios, condensed milk and oranges for breakfast. Earl wanted to see the site of the old logging camp and he thought his leg would be up to it. We just finished eating and the three fox pups come running from the south. As soon as they see Earl, they stopped and started to circle around us. They eventually sat down, keeping an eye on Earl. Earl cannot believe his eyes. The pups have clearly made an impression on him. The pups eventually leave and so do we.

## June 29, 1948 - Late.

We went to the sluice dam site and crossed the stream on one of the 12" x 12" timbers. We climb the hill and come to the logging camp site. Dad and I had only found one building and we are pretty sure it is the blacksmith shop as we found oxen shoes, chain parts and other non-descript pieces of iron.

Earl stood inside the building as we had it marked off. He didn't say anything for many minutes. He turned from time to time but seemed to be trying to picture what went on in this building. Finally, he seemed to be satisfied that he got a good picture in his mind of this building and what could have gone on there. He said his uncle was a blacksmith and was just trying to picture where the forge was, where the anvil was and the stall where he would have put shoes on horses and oxen. We tried to picture where the other two buildings were located. We thought we found two possible sites and since we did not have the magnet, it would have been futile to search for evidence.

By this time, Earl said we better head back as his leg was beginning to act up.

We slowly made our way back to camp and I had plenty of time to get my bag put together and meet Dad's train at 4:47 p.m. This is the first time I met his Monday train. He had a bag for me also and it contained a letter from Savannah. Wow! Mom had some cookies, condensed milk and oranges in the bag. When I got to camp, Earl was stretched out on the ground and I think he had been sleeping. No doubt he didn't get a good nights sleep either night so far. I decide that we can each have a can of Spam for supper and give the trout the day off.

After supper I opened Savannah's letter. There is SWAK on the flap of the letter and I still don't know what it means. Savannah said they had visited the White House and the President was not in. They went to watch both the Senate and Congress. She said they will leave for home the next day and she will meet me by the big pine by late morning on July 2nd. She is anxious to get home, but she has really enjoyed the trip.

Earl and I sat around and talked after supper. I mostly listened because I didn't want to pry into Earls past. I thought if I am willing to listen maybe he will be able to get rid of some of the things that are haunting him. Maybe he just needs lots of time with no great expectations on him except by himself.

I had given a great amount of thought about Earl and his smoking. He certainly doesn't smoke very much. Maybe he could have one cigarette here in camp just before we turn in. Nobody will be around to smell the smoke and find the camp. Tonight I told Earl about that and he thought for a long time and then said, "I can tell you have given this much thought. I appreciate you letting me light up before we turn in. I may take you up on that, but for now I respect why you don't want me to smoke in camp and I won't. You see, I didn't smoke when I went in the service. Many of my buddies smoked and I just started. I eventually used it as a crutch and reached for a smoke when I was stressed. Smoking a cigarette brings back a flood of memories about lots of my buddies that got killed, or badly wounded. I am trying to stop smoking so I can stop seeing my dead or wounded buddies." Earl didn't say anything for twenty minutes. "When we landed on Iwo Jima, I knew there would be casualties. I was not prepared for seeing thousands of Marines lying dead or wounded on the beach. I am still having a very difficult time dealing with all that death. All these young men with their lives ahead of them just snuffed out."

Earl sat there for twenty minutes and then said he was going to turn in. He thanked me for a wonderful day. By now we could hear the tree frogs, frogs in the small swamp and the three owls started talking. In a few minutes, we heard the screechy, scratchy song of the little owl in the branches above us. We could hear something snorting just west of camp. It snorted several times and then ran away crashing in the underbrush. It must have been a deer.

### June 30, 1948 - Early.

I did not hear Earl in the night. I did hear the raccoon climb up the tree toward the food pail. I got up and with my flashlight and the twelve foot pole I had for that purpose, I pushed the little bandit off the tree. He landed with a thud and ran off. We wake up to rain. It looks like we will hang around camp today. Earl rolls out and we eat Cheerios, condensed milk and oranges for breakfast. I hear the kingfisher by the stream. We can hear the cuckoo with its sad song. All at once, the three fox pups run from the south. This time they come right in around us and each one took turns looking in our tents. I held out some Cheerios and one finally came up and smelled it, then grabbed it. I put some more out and one more came and smelled and grabbed them. The third one would not come in. I realize that we should not be trying to tame these wild foxes. It seems more like they are trying to tame us. After about fifteen minutes, they all laid down in a heap and went to sleep about forty feet from us. They didn't seem to mind getting wet.

All at once, one of the little owls came flying down and landed on a dead limb about fifteen feet from me. It sat there for about thirty seconds and then it swooped down and pounced on something in the pine needles and leaves. In a few seconds it flew up to the branch and it had a mouse. Earl said, "This is quite the nature spot. You are fortunate to be able to do what you are doing."

**June 30, 1948 - Late.**

The rain stopped by midday, but the woods were wet. We hung around camp and by mid-afternoon, I decided to tie on the Mepps French Spinner #2 and try to catch trout out of the beaver pond. Earl did not have hip boots so he could not cross the stream, or wade out in the pond, without getting wet. Since he only had one pair of shoes, he realized that he could not go with me. I got to the pond and waded out. I had come up with a plan to be able to cast the spinner with my fly rod by keeping the fly line spread out by my feet. I would pull the spinner in by taking up line so I could keep the spinner at about two feet deep. The first cast went out about forty feet. I began to take up line and, Bang! I got a hard hit and a nice trout jumped out of the water, but it was hooked and I landed it, a nice fat eleven inch brook trout. Into the creel it went. The next two casts produced nothing. I cast to a different spot and caught a nine and one-half inch brookie. Several more casts produced nothing. I decided to let the spinner sink deeper before retrieving it. I barely started retrieving it and got a hard hit. This was a big fish! I could not hold it as it ran to my right. The fish stayed deep and I could not raise it. It made a run to my left and went into shallower water and near some cattails growing there. I tried to keep it away and could not. It got behind the cattails and I figured I would lose it. I kept pressure on the fish and it moved away from the cattails, but kept going away from me. I played out lots of line but the fish ran behind a clump of cattails. The fish stopped and I kept some pressure on it. This went on for about five minutes. Finally, it responded to my pressure and came out from behind the cattails. It slowly swam towards my right and I kept taking up line. Now I could see this trout and it looked like seventeen to nineteen inches. The fish appeared to be tired out and I kept bringing it near me. Finally, I was able to grab the landing net which was stuck in the mud beside me.

I shortened up my grip on the fly rod and brought this beauty closer. I reached out with the net and the fish was nearly in it when it gave a mighty thrash and the spinner pulled out and nearly hit me as it went flying. The big fish just laid in the water exhausted. I could have netted it, but I would have measured it and released it anyway. Besides, this fish put up a hard fight and earned its freedom. The fish slowly began to move its tail and turn toward the deeper water. It slowly swam away and down and was soon out of sight. I was happy that I had a chance to fight this beauty. It gave me a wonderful feeling to feel the power of the fish. I decided that the two trout in my creel would be enough for supper tonight.

When I got to camp, Earl was sitting on one of the campstools. He told me, "I went up to the tracks to have a cigarette but there was a rip track crew working just north of the trail. They must have been replacing some ties. Anyway, I stayed in the woods as I didn't want these guys to see me. I ran into one of their crews down by Eau Claire and they thought I was a hobo and they gave me a hard time. That really bothered me and I didn't want this crew to think I was a hobo, too."

I could tell Earl was upset. I told him about losing the big trout. He thought I should have netted it anyway and brought it back to camp. I told him that there would have been more meat than we could eat at one meal, because I already had two nice trout in my creel.

Earl seemed to agree with me but I still think he thinks it is a bad idea to catch fish and let them go again. He wanted to know more about the beaver pond so I told him that tomorrow we would cross on the sluice dam timbers and we would go to the beaver pond. I would take my fly rod, creel and net, plus my hip boots as I thought Earl might be able to put them on and he could fish. I had Earl try on one of the boots and it fit, so that is our plan.

We got a fire going to boil water and fry the trout. Earl made a cup of coffee and I could tell he wanted to talk. He said, "The war was very hard on me. We trained hard and we had a good outfit, a top notch outfit. I really enjoyed the training and interacting with the other guys. We were very serious but there was a fair amount of horseplay, especially in the evening. We had guys from nearly every state. Some had never been very far from their homes and many were homesick after a few weeks.

We had men from many walks of life, many different religions, many nationalities but most of the men were white-skinned. Many different accents were spoken and three or four men could only speak a little English. We all had trouble getting used to different accents and new terms used in our training. If we made mistakes, we could expect to draw extra duty like KP. Depending on the mistakes being made it could mean extra marching, push-ups, sit-ups or barrier running. All of it was supposed to make us a close knit fighting unit that could rely on each other in battle. There were a few men that got picked on by some others. There were fights from time to time, but for the most part we got along quite well. For sure we were all united in our efforts to be a top fighting unit. In no way would any differences prevent us from defeating the enemy."

"Eventually," he continued, "we all looked on each other as an important cog in a well oiled fighting machine. Each of us had important responsibility in our squad and we had to rely on each other for our very lives. We had developed a closeness for each other far beyond anything I had ever experienced before. Perhaps it was the fact that we were training for events that would be so dangerous that some, or many of us, may lose our lives."

Earl stopped talking and didn't say anything for several minutes. He got up off his camp stool and walked down to the stream and stood looking into the water. He stood by the stream for at least twenty minutes. I decided to fry the trout and get supper ready. When the meal was ready, I called Earl and told him supper was ready. For about one minute, he just stood there and then he came and ate the trout with me. He had a strange, far away look on his face. I could tell that Earl was in a wrestling match with events leading up to the war as well as the war itself. Perhaps events after the war are weighing even heavier than other events on this veteran who obviously had been in a place that few of us have had to endure. The events of the past have taken a terrible toll on this mans being and he is struggling to overcome those ghostly memories so he can go on with his life. I don't know how to help him except be a good listener and be a good friend.

**July 1, 1948 - Early.**

I heard the owls again last night. Could also hear night hawks and frogs in the small swamp. No tree frogs and no saw-whet owls. As Earl and I ate breakfast, a mother partridge and her brood of eleven chicks came into view, moving along the stream and headed right toward the campsite. We could see them all foraging for insects, buds and any other source of food. Eventually they veered toward the stream and in about thirty minutes were out of sight. I have been told that at night, or during a rainfall, the mother partridge holds out her wings and all the chicks huddle together under the wings. That certainly sounds like a family event. These chicks were big enough that they may have been able to fly.

We finish breakfast and clean up. We head to the sluice dam with the fishing gear and my hip boots. We arrive at the northwest side of the beaver pond. Earl was very impressed with the pond and then we walked on to the beaver dam and he was really impressed. The dam was about four and one-half feet high and about sixty-five feet long. That was a big project for these beavers. We continued to the southwest part of the pond and Earl put my hip boots on. He got the fly rod ready, took the creel and net and followed the trail of sticks in the pond. He reached the end of the sticks and unlimbered the fly rod with the Mepps French Spinner on it.

The first two or three casts were duds. Earl caught on and the next cast went out about forty feet and as he took up line retrieving the spinner, he got a hard hit. Earl set the hook and right now a nice trout jumped about one and a half feet out of the water. It appeared to be about twelve inches long. Earl took up line and decided to walk back to shore to land this beauty. He went back and got the net and continued toward me. He tossed me the net and went back to fighting the trout which by now was very tired. He guided the trout to the net and I scooped it up and measured it. I gave it to Earl to put in the creel with some fresh grass. Earl was all smiles. He had caught many fish, but this was the first trout he caught, other than on the Brule River, and it was the first fish since before he went into the Marines. He was happy.

Earl waded out and started casting again. On his third cast, I told him to let it sink deeper before retrieving the spinner. He just started taking up line and he got a hard hit. This fish stayed deep for several seconds. It moved to the right and, all at once, it jumped out of the water and was shaking like crazy. It looked to be larger than the first fish. It fell back in the water and ran to the left. All at once, it jumped out of the water again. Earl kept pressure on the trout and it dove deep one time and he could not take up line fast enough. When he finally got caught up, the line was empty. The trout had gotten away. Earl felt elated! He really enjoyed feeling the power of this nice trout. "So what if it got away. It fought hard." Earl said. I guess Earl and I feel about the same about a hard fighting fish getting another chance to return to its home.

Earl waded out and cast again. He caught a nine inch brookie and in a few minutes caught an eight and one-half inch brookie. Several more casts produce no fish and we decided to head back to camp. As we neared the dam, all at once, it sounded like someone tossed a large rock in the water. Earl had a strange, scared look on his face and I said, "That is a beaver slapping the water with its tail as a warning." Apparently we had surprised it as it swam near the dam. He returned the favor by surprising us.

We crossed the amazing beaver dam and then crossed the stream on the big beams of the sluice dam. We arrived in camp and sat down. I told Earl about Savannah and he seemed somewhat surprised and seemed somewhat depressed. When I told him I would be meeting Savannah tomorrow, he acted like he didn't want to share me with her. This is a new angle on Earl and this camp.

Earl seemed withdrawn during supper. I did not try to talk to him. I decided to take some of the warm water and wash up all over my body. This would be the first 'sponge bath' since I started camping. With Savannah coming tomorrow I did not want to smell like some dirty old man. Since I started my camping adventure, I washed up regularly and used deodorant and changed my under clothes and clothes regularly. Mom insisted on that. I can tell that Earl is still wrestling with the demons of his past. I think he really enjoyed fishing today, but somehow, news that I would be meeting Savannah threw him a curve ball.

I was working on this diary when Earl asked if he could smoke a cigarette in camp. I said he could, so he lit up and I could sense that he wanted to talk. I was right.

Earl moved his camp stool closer to me and said, "I am really struggling with my future. I feel that I have found a home with you. We have gotten along very well and I really hoped I could stay with you until you break camp. I am really anxious to meet your mom and dad as they must be  very nice people. I had a far out thought that they may help me to find a job and a place to live in Spooner."

"It really would be asking a lot of all three of you, but I don't seem to be able to work things out myself. I have been doing better the past two or three days and I had a wonderful day today. When you told me about your friend, Savannah, it seemed like a big dark cloud dropped on me and I slid backwards. I don't seem to be able to stand up to some of the war memories and when I thought I might have to share you with Savannah, it really sank my ship."

As Earl spoke, he seemed to be more upbeat than when he

started. By the time he finished the cigarette, he seemed more at ease and I could sense that he had more to tell me but he sat quietly for at least five minutes. By now it was nearly dark and I spoke and asked Earl, "Does having a cigarette help you wrestle with the past?" Earl did not answer for several minutes, but then he said, "You already know that I started smoking after I joined the Marines. Nearly all of us smoked and it is one of the things in my life that is the same now as it was on Iwo Jima. That is about the only thing that is the same. When I light up a cigarette, I only think good thoughts. On Iwo Jima we didn't smoke if we were fighting, only if we had a pause in the action. Those pauses were a godsend to all of us and we would light up. Invariably, we got the orders to move out and it turned out that it meant more of my comrades got wounded or killed. Having the next cigarette kept me going. It was a goal - survive to have another cigarette."

By now it was dark and the frogs, owls and other night critters were joining the fireflies as they all went about their nightly rituals. Earl spoke after three or four minutes. He said, "I really want to smoke another cigarette but I am not going to. I know that I am using the cigarettes as a crutch and I need to deal with my past without falling back on smoking. Besides, you have a big day tomorrow with Savannah so let's hit the hay."

I had never been around anyone with serious war stress. I had heard the term 'shell shocked' and I wonder if that is what Earl is struggling with. I certainly will try to do whatever I can to help this brave veteran overcome his problems. It was very interesting that he is hoping Mom and Dad could help him find a job and a place to live.

Somehow, I think Earl and I will be companions for more than a few days.

**July 2, 1948 - Early.**

Savannah comes today! Shortly after I crawled out of my tent, a small object landed by my right foot. It fell from up in the huge pine tree and it looked like a small pellet about three-eighth of an inch long and less than a quarter of an inch in diameter. I picked it up after looking closely at it. Earl saw me looking at it in my hand and he looked at it and saw that it was an owl pellet - most likely from our little saw-whet owl friend up in this tree.

We looked closely at it and could see lots of fine hair. We broke it open and found mouse bones, claws and other material. Earl said, "Owls can't digest these things so from time to time they burp up these pellets." We looked up in the tree and sure enough, there sat our little friend up about thirty feet. We looked some more and saw the three babies a little higher in the tree.

Earl seems fine today. I asked him what he planned to do today. He planned to cross the stream at the sluice dam and spend the day at the beaver pond. He wanted to see the beavers and he knows there are lots of ducks there. We ate breakfast and I put on my hip boots and took my fly rod, creel and landing net and headed for the big pine. Boy, I was nervous, but excited.

I got to the big pine and sat on the bank up stream from the hole. I kept a watch on the trail upstream and finally about midmorning, Savannah comes into view. I stood up and moved to meet her. I have wondered what we would

do when we met.  I was very unsure on what to do.
Anyway, we waved at each other when she was about one
hundred feet away.  We spoke and said "Hi" as we got
closer and then Savannah reached her hand out to me to
shake hands, which we did.  But then, she pulled me to
her and we hugged.  Wow!  I was sure my face was red.
Boy, she smelled great even with her fishing vest on.

We made small talk and then Savannah reached into her
creel and brought out a box and handed it to me.  She
said, "I bought a present for you - open it up."  I could see
it had 'Zebco' on the box and I knew that was the name of
a company that makes fishing reels.  I opened the box and
saw it was a spinning reel.  I had seen a picture of one in
an outdoor magazine but here was one in my hand.
Savannah said, "You can take your fly rod reel off your
fly rod and put this new reel on, in its place.  It goes on
the under side of the fly rod.  She reached into her creel
again and brought out a little plastic tackle box and
handed it to me.  "Open it," she said.  I did and found
about a dozen spinners in the box.  I picked one up and
saw that it was a Mepps French Spinner made in Antigo,
Wisconsin.  Some had colored spinners, or a bright red or
yellow plastic band on the treble hook.  Some had buck
tail  hair on the treble hook.  All were stamped with a 1, 2
or 3 on the blade of the spinner.

Savannah said,  "Use these if you wish and, in a week or
two, I want to take you to a special place upstream from
here and away from the stream.  You will be amazed by
this series of pools and the trout that are there."

It was my turn.  "What the heck is SWAK on the flap of
the letters you sent me?"  "Silly," she said, "that means

sealed with a kiss." Boy my face must have been red as it certainly felt hot. "While I am making a fool of myself, what is OVELA? Is it some sort of foreign language?" "Silly again. Haven't you heard of Pig Latin?" I said, "I have heard of it but don't know anything about it." "Pig Latin is where you take the first letter of a word, like LOVE and put it at the end of the word and then add the letter A so LOVE is now OVELA. Nick would be ICKNA, Savannah would be AVANNAHSA."

About now I told Savannah that I had two peanut butter and jelly sandwiches, if she was hungry. She said, "I guessed you would provide sandwiches so I brought this." She reached into her creel and produced a bottle of Coca Cola and one of Cream Soda, apparently just new to this area. "Which one do you want?" I said, "Your choice." She chose the Coca Cola so I got the Cream Soda. I must say it was very good.

We had our lunch and Savannah produced a 'Mounds Bar' which we split. That was easy as the bar is already split into two bars. I told Savannah about the nice trout I had caught, some of the large ones I released. She wanted to know about the large landing net so I told her about the size of some of the trout I had hooked or seen. She was excited and wanted to try to catch one or two of these beauties.

The next hole down stream was the steep bank hole. I told Savannah about the fourteen and one-half inch German Brown trout I caught there and I explained that the hole had a sunken log but also ran under the bank. I told her that I had to put a split shot on my line to get the worm down into the hole.

132

Savannah had been watching to see what insects were hatching and decided to tie on a Royal Nymph fly, which she did. She floated the dark colored fly into the left side of the hole and it got swept under the overhang. After about two seconds she felt a strike so she set the hook and I could tell by the bend of her rod that she had a nice fish on. She could not do anything with the fish for about one minute. Finally, it moved under the log and away from Savannah. She was able to turn it to the left when it got to the end of the log. The next thing the fish did was come up out of the water and try to shake the hook out of its mouth. Wow! It was a beauty! At least sixteen inches long and maybe more. It still had plenty of fight and continued to run toward Savannah. She took up line and the fish turned and went straight to the end of the pool. It continued out of that pool and downstream. Savannah was right after it, running beside the stream and stopped about seventy five feet downstream. By now this beauty of a fish was tired and Savannah was able to stop it and hold it. She moved closer and I followed with the net.

As she held the fish in the current, I slipped the net under it and brought it to Savannah. She carefully removed this German Brown trout from the net. We carefully removed the fly and measured this beauty. It was seventeen and one-quarter inches long and Savannah estimated that it weighed about two and one-half pounds. She gently placed this big trout back into the hole where she first felt it bite. She then took out a small notebook and recorded the time, date, bait used and the length and weight of the fish. When this was all done, she said, "That was fun. The next trout is yours."

The next hole is what I call the northeast hole. The

stream curves to the left but for whatever reason, there is a four foot deep hole on the right side of this hole. I put on a worm and start playing out line thirty-five feet above the hole. I have one split shot on the leader to get the worm down near the bottom of the hole.

I make one pass through the hole and nothing happened. I take up line and float the worm more to the right and this time I feel a tap on the line. I take up some slack and feel another tap so I set the hook. I could feel a good fish and in about two seconds, I saw it as it jumped out of the water as it came toward me. I could not keep the line tight and the trout was able to spit the hook out and was gone. Savannah said, "It was at least fifteen inches and maybe sixteen. It looked like a brookie."

The next nice hole is right by camp and I call it the big sweep. Water deflects to the left as it hits a large log slanting out into the stream. This has caused a large overhang on the left side of the stream. Savannah thinks the 'Royal Nymph' will still be a good choice of flies so she begins playing out line as we get near the big sweep. The first pass produces no action, neither does the second. Savannah decides to change flies and ties on a number 12 gnat. She played out line and just past the log she gets a hit. It is a nice trout and she is able to land it with no trouble. It is an eleven and one-half inch brook trout. She carefully removed the hook and gently released it back in the stream. Since this is a long run, Savannah stepped up to the log and played out line very close to the left edge of this pool. She had about forty-five feet of line out when she felt a fish. She took up slack and set the hook. Right now there was a huge splash as a very large trout went airborne. It appeared to be a least twenty inches long. It ran right up toward Savannah and she could not take up line fast enough. When she got the slack up, the fish was not on the line anymore.

"WOW!" she said. "That is the biggest trout I have ever had on the line." I told her that the camp was just up the bank and to the left. "Let's take a break."

We climbed up to camp and she immediately saw Earl's tent. I told her, "Grab a camp stool and I will tell you about Earl." I just started telling Earl's story when we could see Savannah's Mom and Dad fishing downstream. We waved at them and told them to come into camp.

Elon and Kathy climbed the bank to the camp. Greetings were exchanged and then Savannah told her mom and dad about the large trout she had on the line a few minutes ago. She said, "It is in the pool just below this bank, waiting for someone to catch it."

I noticed that Elon had a fishing rod different that a fly rod. I asked about it and he answered, "This is a spinning rod." I noticed that it was a Mepps French Spinner on the end of the line. Elon said, "The owners of the Mepps lures is a good friend of mine and they have asked me to use their lures and do some promotional work." I told him about using a Mepps spinner at the beaver pond and had a seventeen to nineteen inch trout about to be netted and it got off. That was using my fly rod and fly line. I am anxious to use the spinning reel that Savannah gave me.

Kathy Casey said, "I talked to our neighbor, Margaret Burns, and she told me all about her catching her foot on a

135

root and falling in the pool by this camp. She really appreciated all the help you gave her to get out of the pool and up to your camp. You stayed up all night and massaged her leg and then spent several hours helping her to her car. She could tell you were getting tired by the time the two of you finally reached her car. She was really impressed that you figured out how to drive her car and got a little chuckle out of getting stuck going up the rocky hill. But you backed down and got a run at it and made it up the hill. Your plan to stop at the body shop and ask someone to take her to the doctor worked just fine. She spent some time in the hospital and then was able to drive her car home and has since recovered and is like new. She plans to look you up after you get home. She really had great praise for you."

Elon and Kathy decided to fish down to the 'sluice dam hole' and would pick Savannah up on the way upstream. They stayed on the west side of the stream until they were below the long hole that had a big trout that Savannah lost. Elon wanted to cast upstream and see how that went. It wasn't very long after they left that we heard a shout 'WOW'. Elon got a very strong strike and it was at least seventeen or eighteen inches long. The fish jumped and spit the spinner out, but Elon was impressed.

Savannah and I stayed in camp and I told her about Earl. She was very sympathetic toward his plight. She also knew of a veteran that lived near them in Antigo, that also was having a very difficult time dealing with events of the war. I had told Savannah that I would try to help Earl anyway I could and hoped my mom and dad would try to help also. We may not be able to be of much help to Earl. Savannah said, "It looks like he enjoys fishing. Is there anyway he can get some equipment to fish with? How about a license?" I said, "I will meet Dad's train tomorrow and give him a note asking for him to buy a fly rod and reel, a creel and a pair of hip boots. I need to find out what size. He could bring them with him when he and Mom visit this coming Sunday. I will ask Dad to see about getting a fishing license for Earl. I think I can pay for all of these as I still have some funds left. I will ask Earl if this would be alright with him."

Savannah asked if I was going to do anything special for the 4th of July. I told her that I had no plans. I certainly didn't have any fireworks and besides, lighting fireworks in this forest would be dangerous. Savannah said, "It's too bad you have to meet your dad's train or you could come with us to our cabin and celebrate the 4th there."

I said, "That is a nice gesture, but what about Earl? He would be in camp all by himself. If it is OK with Earl, could you bring me back by Sunday morning?"

Savannah said, "I think we could, I will ask Dad if we could do that." I said, "I could call Mom and Dad from a phone and ask them to bring the fishing things for Earl and anything else I need. They could bring that with them Sunday afternoon. I think it may work out if it is alright with Earl. He was going to the beaver pond for the day and if he doesn't come back soon, I need to go looking for him."

We talked about Earl's injury, his activities since his release from the hospital and that he wanted to settle in Spooner, not Superior where he grew up. I told Savannah about catching and releasing several nice trout. I told her about what my dad said when there is frost warnings and the cranberry marsh floods the berries to prevent damage from the frost. Most of the water is pumped back into the reservoir behind the dam but some is released and floods the stream. Savannah knew where the cranberry marsh was and she seemed to understand about the flooding and pumping the water back. I told her that when the flood occurs the fish go crazy and I want to be able to try for that big trout you had on this afternoon, or one of several others that I know about. I wonder if my equipment, and my skill level, is up to the task of fighting and landing a twenty inch trout in this small stream. I was really looking forward to trying.

No sign of Earl, so I told Savannah I would go looking for him. Hopefully I will be back soon and off I went. I waded the stream and headed toward the northeast and was at the beaver ponds south side in ten minutes. I called Earl's name, but had no response. I headed to my left and soon arrived at the beaver dam. Again I called for Earl and again no response. I looked for any sign that anyone had been there and I found evidence the someone, or something had pressed down the grass and it seemed to be going to the northeast. About then I hear someone yell NICK! I looked toward the northwest and saw Elon and Kathy coming toward me. They were fishing at the sluice dam hole which is only about a hundred yards from the beaver dam.

I explained that I was looking for Earl to see if it was alright to spend Friday and Saturday with you and Savannah. "I am looking for him now. Have you seen a 25 year old man today?" Elon replied, "We have not." Now I was getting concerned. Did Earl get lost? Once you get away from the stream, or beaver pond, there are many, many acres of woods.

Elon and Kathy wanted to know if they could help. I thought for awhile and said, "He may have been trying to find the site of the old logging camp which is northeast of here. I will head that way, but maybe you two could go north on this ridge, but stay in sight of the stream. Call out Earl's name as you go and I will meet you about one half mile north of here in about thirty to forty minutes. Good luck." Off we went, calling for Earl as we went.

I found my blaze marks and followed it to the old logging camp. I had given up trying to follow the mashed down vegetation. It was too inconsistent. I arrived at the old campsite and I carefully looked for any sign of foot travel. There was none, but all at once I got a very faint smell of cigarette smoke. It was so faint I wasn't positive I had smelled it. The slight breeze in the woods was coming from the northwest, or at least it seemed to come from there. I headed northwest, carefully sniffing the air as I went. I went about a hundred yards and had not smelled any cigarette smoke. I continued to call Earl's name and, then all at once, I smelled cigarette smoke again. It seemed to still be coming from the northwest. I continued calling and moving toward the northwest. Moving in this direction should put me very near Elon and Kathy in about another quarter of a mile or less. I shouted and listened and got no response. I continued sniffing, shouting and listening. After about two hundred yards, I smelled cigarette smoke again, this time it was more distinct.

I shouted and continued walking and came to a steep

ravine that ran at right angles to my route. I stopped on the edge of the ravine and shouted for Earl. I heard a faint response that sounded like 'here'. I looked but could not see anyone. I called again and again I heard 'here'. It sounded like it came from my left and down in the ravine. I headed down toward where I thought I had heard the sound from. After about forty yards, I saw where the leaves on the ground had been ruffed up and then I saw Earl curled up behind a big log. He was on the north side of a large red oak tree that had died and fell over. I approached Earl and he looked at me with a strange, very strange look on his face.

"Captain Miller, better get down, the Japs are all over this valley. They shot Carew, Turnquist and Mast. All dead, Sir, better get down." I could tell that Earl had something very bad going on in his mind. I moved up and put my hand on his shoulder and he looked up and said, "I knew you would come for me, Captain. I knew it! Where is the rest of the outfit?" I told him, "They are waiting for us back at camp and we need to get back there as soon as we can. Are you ready, Burke?" Earl replied, "Yes, Captain, lets get back to camp. What about Carew, Turnquist and Mast? We better take them back with us, don't you think?" I said, "Soldier, they are safe for now and we will come back for them, but for now we need to return to camp."

About then, I heard Elon call out Earl's name. "Captain Miller, don't you hear that, the Jap's are calling to me. They want me to go to them and then they will kill me or torture me and then kill me like they did to Jajuski, Roberts, Snellson and French. Captain get down." I said, "Soldier, that is one of our unit trying to find you. We have driven the enemy away and it is safe to leave and return to camp. I will go and tell the rest of our outfit where you are. Stay put and I will be back soon. The fighting is done for now, Earl. Rest for a while."

I hustled toward Elon's voice and in a few minutes found Elon and Kathy. I told them about Earl and what he seemed to be going through. "He thinks I am Captain Miller, who I heard him speak of once in the night a few nights ago. He must be reliving a terrible event on Iwo Jima. We need to be very careful how we deal with Earl. He is acting very, very strange. He thinks you are part of his outfit coming to rescue him. Perhaps Kathy could perform her duties as a nurse to try to focus his thoughts and emotions away from what he is going through now." Elon agreed and wondered if Earl could walk and I did not know. We decided we better go to Earl and try to get him back to camp, which is about a mile away.

We went back to Earl and I told him, "This is Sergeant Casey and Nurse Kathy. Kathy will look you over to see if you have any serious injuries." Kathy felt of his forehead, asked him to move his arms and legs, stand up and she felt his back, shoulders, stomach, neck and asked a few questions. She then asked Earl, "Are you ready to go back to camp?" "Yes, ma'am, I am ready," he replied.

I said, "I will lead and watch out for the enemy. Nurse Kathy, follow Earl and Sergeant Casey, keep a watch for anyone trying to attack from the rear." We headed out and by now it was early evening so we needed to move at a good steady pace. Earl seemed much better and despite his injured leg, was able to move at a pretty good clip. I wondered what Savannah was thinking. Poor girl, must be wondering what is going on.

We crossed the stream on the timbers at the sluice dam and were on the home stretch. Earl kept talking about us, saying, "We are going back to pick up Carew, Turnquist and Mast. They were my buddies and we need to take good care of their bodies. Someone needs to send their things home and write a letter to their mom and dad. I went home on leave with Carew once. He is a Wisconsin boy. We went shining deer one night and I saw some monster bucks. Carew was one of the very best."

We arrived in camp and Savannah was relieved. She gave me a big hug and then I introduced her to Earl. Right now Earl seemed to revert back to a normal man. He was very impressed with Savannah. We had a discussion and I asked Earl what had happened. He said, "I went looking for the old logging camp. I got lost and started down the ravine and all of a sudden I was under attack and I was part of a platoon that had Carew, Turnquist and Mast in it. They were killed and I was able to get behind a big log, but I was scared, all I could do was smoke. I realize now that my three buddies were killed, but it was on Iwo Jima about four years ago. I wanted Captain Miller to come and get me out of the danger that I was in, so when Nick showed up, I latched on to him. I was really glad to see you, Nick."

Elon and Kathy had talked and now they had a proposal. Elon said, "How about Earl and Nick coming with us to our cabin by Birchwood and spend Friday and Saturday there. We can bring you back by Sunday morning." "Earl, how does that sound to you?" I asked. Earl responded, "I don't want to put anyone out, but these folks do seem like very nice people. If you think our stuff will be safe here, it is fine with me." Elon asked me, "Would you both like to spend two days with us at our cabin?" I said, "I need to hide my fishing gear and my gun, but I would take my diaries along. Yes, that sounds like a very nice time." Elon told me later that Earl needed to get away from the big woods. He just had a mental relapse and perhaps a change of scenery will help. Earl really is having a hard go of things.

By this time, it was about an hour before sundown. We secured the tents, hid the fishing gear, except for the hip boots which we needed to cross the stream. The .22 rifle was a different deal because it needed to stay dry. Finally, I decided to keep it in its case and put it under the floor of the tent off to the side where I kept canned food, clothes, etc.

We all headed toward the stream, but in different places so it would not look like people had come to the stream in one place. My boots would fit Earl, so he put them on, crossed the stream and Elon brought them back to me. I put the boots on and carried my shoes and my diaries and crossed the stream and joined the rest of the group.

Elon went ahead with the idea that if he saw a trout fisherman he would come back and we would take a different route around the fisherman. We did not meet anyone and within about half hour we reached Casey's car, a 1947 Dodge four door. The Casey's loaded their fishing gear and hip boots in the ample trunk. We all climbed into the car, Savannah next to the door and I sat in the middle. Earl sat next to the other door and remarked, "This is the first car I have been in since before

I joined the Marines." He said, "I am impressed as to how nice it is. Thanks for inviting me to visit your place."

We started south on the dirt road, leaving Beaver Brook behind us. In about two minutes, we could see the cranberry marsh with the dam visible in the distance. We went near the small buildings housing some workers and there were the young Indian couple sitting outside their building. Earl asked Elon, "Can you stop for a couple of minutes?" Elon said, "Of course," and he stopped. Earl got out and went to the young couple. They greeted him warmly. After about two minutes, I decided to get out of the car and greet Little Dove and Walking Bear. I encouraged Elon, Kathy and Savannah to come and meet this nice couple. I was greeted warmly and Little Dove wanted to know if I had her gift yet. I reached into my pocket and produced the rabbit foot with the attached beads. Little Dove seemed very pleased and both were very happy to meet Elon, Kathy and Savannah. Little Dove was very excited and when she met Savannah she held her hand up and ran into her house. In a few seconds she emerged with a rabbit foot with attached leather and beads and presented it to Savannah. She told Savannah it was a gift of friendship. She apologized to Elon and Kathy that she did not have anymore gifts at the present, but if she did she would surely have given them each one. About this time, Earl produced a rabbit foot with leather and beads from his pocket. It was a happy few minutes, but Elon said we must be on our way.

We said good-bye and climbed into the car and headed south. Presently we went up a very steep winding road. Kathy said, "Wow, this would be a wonderful sliding hill in the winter." We all agreed. With the three of us in the back seat, it was crowded and I was up against Savannah and it felt great! After about twenty-five minutes, Elon drove into the driveway at their cabin and by now it was nearly dark. Elon had driven on so many roads that I would have not been able to navigate back to Beaver Brook.

This was a long day, filled with unexpected events. We unloaded and went into the cabin which was nice, but not elaborate. Kathy immediately started frying bacon and eggs, as well as making toast. That really got my mouth watering. It was many hours since lunch.

We finished that wonderful meal and Savannah and I did up the dishes while Elon, Kathy and Earl visited. Savannah washed the dishes and I dried, but once she reached out and put a gob of soap suds on my head. That was cool, but then she dried her hands and grabbed my head and wiped the suds off. I put my arm around her waist to steady myself as some of the suds had run onto my face. Savannah holding my head and me holding her produced an unfamiliar feeling, but a feeling that I didn't want to stop.

The cabin was nice, but only had two bedrooms. Earl and I would sleep on sleeping bags on the rug in front of the large fireplace. Earl seemed very normal, but deep down I wondered if an episode like today could happen again. For today, I am tired and I have stayed up long after all the others went to bed, but I need to record today's events in this diary. Good night.

## July 3, 1948 - Early.

I slept like a log. We had a nice breakfast of cold cereal, orange juice and coffee. Earl really enjoyed the fresh coffee. I had already asked Earl if he wanted my dad to get him a fly rod and reel, a creel and hip boots. Dad would get the proper fly line, some leaders, hooks, sinkers and a bait box to carry worms with him as he fishes.

We discussed the fishing license requirements and Kathy called her brother, the game warden, that also has a cabin on the same lake and inquired about the license. Her brother, John, the 'Brush Cop' said that a sportsman club in Taylor County wanted him to buy any kind of license, hunting or fishing, for any World War II veteran that needed one. Kathy said he had licenses with him and since all three of the men were going bass fishing this morning, Earl would get a license.

I used the Casey's phone and called Mom and Dad. I told Dad what I wanted for Earl and he said he would try to get all of it and bring it with him when they visit the camp on Sunday, July 5th. They are very anxious to meet Earl and are really looking forward to visiting the camp. I asked them to bring five packs of Camel cigarettes for Earl. That produced a long pause, but finally agreement was made.

## July 3, 1948 - Late.

John, the 'Brush Cop' and his wife and three daughters came over by mid-morning. The warden was tall and quite athletic. He looked like a basketball player and I think he did play some. He was better known as a boxer and Elon said he had used his boxing skill on a few occasions to subdue someone that violated hunting, trapping and fishing laws. All three men got in Elon's boat and pushed off in search of large mouth bass. They had extra gear for Earl and were well equipped with jitterbugs of many colors, including a bright yellow one, a red headed mouse, a bass oreno and night crawlers.

Savannah and I had planned to 'shoot some baskets' at the basketball hoop in the yard. With the visiting girls, we decided to include the two older ones, Mary and Helen, and play a game. The youngest daughter, Beth, was only three years old so she stayed by her mother.

Mary and I played Savannah and Helen and both sides were fairly evenly matched. Savannah was a very good basketball player and was easily better than me. The game went on for at least twenty-five minutes and the score was tied. Mary made up for my lack of skill at this game. Mary made a high pass to me near the basket and I tried to catch it, but I fell into some blackberry brambles and really got scratched by the pickers. My left arm was really bleeding from several long scratches. Savannah took me by the hand and we ran to the cabin. I stood outside while Savannah went and got a bowl of warm soapy water and she washed my arm so we could see where the scratches were. After a few minutes, the bleeding stopped so nurse Savannah got the Methyolate and painted up each scratch. That stung for awhile, but when it got dried Savannah got a roll of gauze to start wrapping my arm. In order to get started, she needed the tape so she reached over my arm to get the tape off a small table. Quite by accident her left breast brushed against my hand and I had the strangest feeling sweep

over me.  My face felt hot and it was probably red.
Savannah looked at me and asked if I was OK.  WOW!
That girl was getting to me!  I felt embarrassed for
accidentally touching her breast but - - it sure turned
something on in me.

We decided that we better not continue with the
basketball game but we could play HORSE and we did.
Guess what, I came in last and Savannah was first.  By
now it was lunch time so we headed for the cabin.  The
three fishermen were still out on the lake so we ate
without them.

At lunch, Kathy said that Margaret Burns had called and
wondered if I was with the Casey's.  Her cabin was two
doors north and she thought she saw me there.  Anyway,
she invited Savannah and me to come over sometime that
afternoon as she wanted to see me.  That was fine with me
because I wondered how her leg was, besides she was a
very nice lady, very much like my mom.

Savannah held my hand for part of the walk to Margaret's
house.  That produced another 'interesting feeling'.  I
guess that is part of growing up, but I was struggling with
my feelings for Savannah.  Margaret greeted us and gave
me a big hug - wow!  She looked great and said her leg
had completely healed.  She said she had thought about
that night when the injury to her leg occurred near my
camp.  She explained what happened to Savannah
including how we slowly got from the camp to her car.
She told about my driving the 1937 Ford and taking her to
the body shop where the men working there took her to
the hospital in Spooner.  She really appreciated all that I
had done for her and she said she stopped at a sport shop

and looked at automatic fly rod reels. I told the clerk, "I need the very best reel in your store, it's for my hero!" She continued, "The clerk reached into a showcase and brought out a South Bend, Oren-O-Matic, balanced reel. I told him to wrap it up. It is for a special fourteen-year-old boy that saved my life."

Margaret reached up on the mantle of the fireplace and took down a small box. She walked up to me and put her left arm around my shoulder and then handed the box to me. I opened the box and there was this beautiful, deep maroon automatic fly rod reel. It was awesome! I had seen these beauties in the Spooner sporting goods store and really admired them, but they were expensive so I just looked but now I had one. I said, "Thanks," and gave Margaret a big hug. We stayed and visited for awhile and then said goodbye and started walking back to Savannah's cabin. I reached out to take Savannah's hand, but she withdrew it. She said, "It looks like you and Margaret get along quite well." I may be inexperienced, but I could tell Savannah did not appreciate Margaret's show of affection toward me.

We walked in silence and confusion. Apparently, Savannah was a little jealous even though Margaret must be at least close to thirty-five years old. Boy, this being a kid is confusing.

The three fishermen were just pulling into the dock as we arrived back at the cabin. All of us kids went to the dock to see what they caught. Elon lifted the stringer and there were several nice bass in the two to four pound range. They caught six big bass that were from four and one-half pounds to seven pounds. They measured them and then released them back into the lake. When asked why they were released, John the 'Brush Cop' said, "Large bass don't taste as good as the ones we kept. All plugs caught bass but the yellow jitterbug was the best bass catcher today." "Earl caught as many as John and I did," said Elon.

Earl volunteered to clean and fillet the bass. Savannah and I volunteered to help and we got started. John and Elon got busy getting a small bonfire going down by the lake. Earl was very good with the fillet knife. Savannah and I each filleted two bass and Earl did six. Savannah took the fillets to Kathy as that was on the menu for tonight. Earl and I cleaned up and buried the remains of the bass and then joined the rest sitting on lawn chairs around the bonfire.

Beth was sitting next to Earl and the three year old asked Earl, "Have you been in the war?" because she saw a small tattoo on his forearm. Earl said, "Yes, I was." And then Beth asked, "Did you get hurt?" Earl said, "Yes, I have been hurt." After a long pause he said, "I was fighting on Iwo Jima and got hit by shrapnel and it tore a big hole in my right leg, up in the thigh. Luckily, Doc Bradley, our corpsman was very close and when I called Corpsman, he was right there and stopped the bleeding and put powder on the wound and wrapped it up. He stayed by me for many minutes, but I lost a great amount of blood and was very weak, almost passing out. I got loaded on a stretcher and two soldiers took me to the beach. Doc Bradley stayed with me for several minutes but then he got called to attend another soldier. I got transported to a hospital ship and eventually to the States. I spent over a year in several hospitals because my leg just would not heal, but here I am."

Elon said, "Doc Bradley helped you?" Earl said, "He was the one." Elon asked, "Is this the Doc Bradley that was one of the flag raisers on Mount Suribachi?" Earl said, "That is the same Doc Bradley." Elon said, "He just moved to Antigo and I have met him. He joined the Antigo Lions Club, of which I am a member." Earl jumped out of his chair and shouted at Elon. "You know Doc Bradley? Is he OK? What is he doing in Antigo?" Elon said, "He works for a mortuary in Antigo and many of us think he will buy it as the owners are elderly and Doc, or John Bradley is a very distinguished and popular guy." Earl said, "I have got to go to Antigo some day and visit Doc. He saved my life and is a regular guy. I saw both of the flags go up on Suribachi as I was about one hundred yards from the second flag. I didn't know who the flag raisers were until many weeks later. I was very sick in several hospitals and finally I saw the famous picture and read the names. Doc was the only one I recognized. I know that Doc, Ira Hayes and Rene Gagnon helped raise huge amounts of money through the sale of war bonds after the war." Now I know more about Earl.

We had a wonderful meal of fried bass fillets, new potatoes, radishes and fresh bread that Kathy baked today. After supper, the kids played and the adults visited until dusk. Then some sparklers were lit and the three girls ran around lighting up the place. Finally, it was dark enough to get out the fireworks, which consisted of three rockets, a handful of small fire crackers and six big, loud firecrackers. Great care was used to light the rockets which went out over the lake and exploded. The little firecrackers exploded all around and finally the six loud bangers were lit and then it was done. By this time it was late enough to call it a day. Savannah did seem to have gotten over whatever was bothering her earlier. She did give me a hug before we said good night. It took me most of an hour to write up the events of today.

## July 4, 1948 - Early.

Holy Cow!! About 4:00 a.m. we heard the loudest, strangest sound coming from the lake. It woke Earl and me up right now. Earl said, "It is loons out on the lake." Man, they were loud. I had seen loons in the water and they are very large. I saw loons fly over three times so far and heard their haunting call, which sounds almost like some one laughing.

## July 4, 1948 - Late.

Savannah changed the dressing on my scratches. Things got going later today. Savannah and I took the bass baits and rods and went bass fishing with the boat. We looked for lily pads, or trees that had fallen into the lake. We would cast the surface plugs near the lilies or tree, wait 15-20 seconds and give the bait a small twitch and bang, the bass would grab the lure and immediately come flying up out of the water. That was exciting. We fished for three hours and caught thirteen bass. The biggest was a fat five pounder and the smallest was twelve inches. We released all of them back in the lake. Savannah and I had a great chance to visit and we did. She wants to take me to the secret pools on the east side of the road that goes over Beaver Brook. We will use Mepps spinners when we fish there. We both hope we can fish in the high water after the cranberry marsh floods the berries to protect against possible frost. I will be able to tell when the water rises. Also I could be suspicious if the night before was cool or cold.

The trick will be to let Savannah and her parents know when that might happen. I told Savannah I could go and see Little Dove and Walking Bear and see if they would be able to call you the night before if the workers at the marsh started flooding the cranberries. It could happen any day, but we should have about two weeks before they flood. Savannah thought that plan might work and they could invite Margaret to fish also. If we each took one of the good holes, we all could have a chance to catch some nice trout. All the big trout would be released, except I wanted to give Little Dove and Walking Bear one or two nice trout for helping contact the Casey's.

Savannah thought the plan was good. She and her parents had to go back to Antigo around the 20th of July and again about August 10th. They would move back to Antigo about August 20th. Savannah was apprehensive about starting high school at a large school like Antigo. There will be lots of kids coming into high school from several rural schools. She will know the kids from the Antigo Junior high school, but she expects one hundred or more new students from the rural schools. Besides that, part of the Menominee Indian reservation is in the Antigo school district so there will be many Indians in school also. Savannah was really looking forward to having Indians in class with her. I could tell that Savannah was concerned about beginning high school. I told her to not think about it and just enjoy the summer. She agreed and then said, "I apologize for the way I reacted when Margaret hugged you. I finally realized how close Margaret came to being in a life threatening circumstance when she got her leg caught on the bank and fell into a pool. Lucky for her you were able to come to her rescue and get her to your camp. Caring for her that night and helping her inch her way to her car was a wonderful, difficult job for you. Your driving her car must have been hilarious, but wonderful. I now can see why she called you her hero. You are my hero also." WOW!

We spent the evening around the bonfire on the beach. John and his family were there and Earl and I were very welcome. Conversation around the fire that night was mostly about how things were normal compared to the war years. Men returned and took back many jobs held by women during the war. 'Rosie, the Riveter' was mentioned. People were happy to be able to buy refrigerators, cars, nylons and not have to deal with the ration books. Many of the veterans took advantage of the GI bill to attend college or get on the farm training. Generally, there was a feeling of happiness and contentment as war time memories faded away.

About midnight people began drifting away from the bonfire. Savannah and I made our way to the cabin and I reached out and took her hand as we walked. As we neared the cabin, Savannah pulled me into a shadowy area by the cabin. She put her arms around me and I did the same. We shared a very nice kiss!! WOW! That made my face feel hot. One more kiss and then we said good night. My heart must have been going like crazy. That girl sure gets me excited.

## July 5, 1948 - Early.

No loons calling during the night last night. A raccoon tried to get the lid off the garbage can and I heard that. Today Earl and I will go back to camp and Mom and Dad will visit at noon. I can hear Kathy in the kitchen and I can smell bacon frying and coffee brewing. The coffee got Earl out of the sleeping bag as he went to get a cup.

## July 5, 1948 - Late.

Elon took Earl and me back to Beaver Brook so we could return to camp. On the way, Elon and Earl visited about the possibility of Earl coming to Antigo and seeing Doc Bradley. Earl really wanted to see Doc, so Elon invited Earl to ride with Kathy, Savannah and him on July 20th. They needed to return to Antigo to oversee some repairs to their house. Elon would see to it that Earl got a chance to visit Doc Bradley. Earl was very excited about the prospect of seeing Doc Bradley again and was very appreciative of the opportunity. Elon opened the trunk and got out a six foot spinning rod and gave it to me. "Good luck," he said.

We got back to camp and everything seemed fine. We got a fire started so we could boil some water to kill any germs. Mom and Dad showed up around noon with lots of food, including her fried chicken along with the fishing gear and cigarettes that had been requested. I introduced Earl to Mom and Dad and they seemed happy to meet him. Earl was very cordial and seemed to really appreciate the fishing gear. Mom seemed to be especially friendly. By now my folks knew Earl was a wounded Marine from the invasion of Iwo Jima. It seemed like they sincerely wanted Earl to be comfortable around them. Both thanked Earl for his military service.

The four of us spent a very enjoyable afternoon visiting. The folks had brought the last two *Spooner Advocate* newspapers so some time was spent discussing events mentioned in the two papers. I got out my new automatic fly rod reel that I got as a gift from Margaret Burns. Mom wanted to know if her leg had healed.

Earl and I told about the past days at the Casey cabin, including the bass fishing. I brought up about Earl being wounded and treated by Doc Bradley and that he lives in Antigo now. Earl was planning to ride to Antigo on July 20th and hopefully could visit Doc Bradley. Mom and Dad both knew about the famous flag raiser who had recently moved to Antigo. They were excited about the possibility of Earl being able to visit Doc.

By late afternoon, Mom and Dad were getting ready to head for home when, all at once, the three more than half grown red fox pups came running from the south, right into camp and looked at and smelled everything. They were noticeably bigger but didn't show any fear of any of us. After about ten minutes, they abruptly left and headed south. Almost on cue, one of the saw-whet owls dropped out of one of the pine trees, grabbed a mouse and flew back up to a lower dead limb about twelve feet from where Mom was sitting. She had never seen one of these little owls and I told her that there may be four more up in these pine trees. We all looked and sure enough, up about twenty-five feet, there they sat, all on the same limb. The three babies were a little smaller than the adult, but not much smaller. I told Mom, "Slowly get up and walk over to the owl, see how close you can get."

She slowly approached the owl and stood about arms length from the owl as it intently looked at her, but swiveled its head to look around from time to time. Mom slowly reached up and touched the limb about one foot from the owl. It just perched there watching Mom and her hand. Mom moved her hand a few inches and the owl took the dead mouse and moved a little further out on the limb. Mom decided to withdraw from the owl and sit down again. About then, one of the owls in the tree let out its screechy-scratchy call, which brought a smile to all of our faces. In about five minutes the owl with the mouse flew up to the rest of the clan and just sat nearby. We assumed that eventually the mouse got shared by all the owls.

We had the remainder of the fried chicken that Mom kept cool in a small ice chest. She also had a strawberry pie that was half eaten for lunch so that was finished also. Mom and Dad gathered up things, including my dirty clothes and some for Earl. I sent two notebooks of my diary with Mom and she said she would not read them, but - "I don't believe you, Mom." Anyway, don't tell anyone. I walked up to the tracks with the folks and told them more about Earl. He wants to live in Spooner, but now that he might meet up with Doc Bradley, he may want to locate at Antigo. Anyway, be on the lookout for any job that may be open.

It took me until dark to write up today's happenings. Good night.

**July 6, 1948 - Early**.

I heard something walking near the tent last night. I also heard it sniffing. I think it was a deer, but - - -. I also heard some howling, way in the distance. That is eerie.

After breakfast, Earl and I got busy and rigged up our fly rods. I had to take the line off my reel and put it on the automatic reel. Once the line was on the reel, I had to twist a small wheel on the side of the reel to put some tension on the springs. As line is pulled out, that winds up the spring so when I want to retract the line, I use my little finger to operate a lever and it reels in the line. That is pretty cool.

**July 6, 1948 - Late**.

We decide to wait until late afternoon to try our new gear. We decided to walk the tracks to the cranberry marsh and visit Little Dove and Walking Bear. We wanted to see if they would be able to call the Casey's if and when the marsh got flooded. We arrived at their shack by late morning and only Little Dove was there, Walking Bear was working with the marsh crew, but he would be home for lunch. Little Dove was very happy to see us and invited us to sit on the bench on the east side of the shack. We visited about many things and Little Dove was very happy to see that Earl was walking much better than the first time she had seen him.

Little Dove explained that about 1910, the owner of the marsh was just getting started and he asked some of their relatives to help with the planting and caring for the new cranberry plants. Their relatives lived in these houses in the summer but now they are the only ones that come in the summer and the other houses have been torn down. All except this one and the one next door. No one has lived in that one for at least five years so it will probably be torn down in the near future.

Walking Bear came home for lunch and we were invited to join them. To refuse would have been in very poor taste so, of course, we accepted their kind invitation for lunch. During lunch we explained our plan to fish for the big trout during the high water if the marsh was flooded. We asked if one of them could call the Casey's, whom they remember of meeting, to tell them that the marsh was flooded.

We explained that we knew most of the water will be pumped back into the reservoir but the remainder of the water is released down stream. They both understood that event as they had seen it several times and yes, they would call the Casey's from a phone at the caretakers house about 200 feet away from their shack. I gave Little Dove the phone number and a dollar to cover the cost of a long distance call. The number was 'long distance' - Birchwood - R-20, or Margaret Burns, Birchwood, R-16. Little Dove knew how to make long distance calls as she calls her parents in Alabama from time to time. Walking Bear wanted Earl to come to work at the marsh now and during the harvest which is usually in September. Earl thanked him for the invitation, but he said he would think about it but he knew that he was going to Antigo on July 20th to visit the man that saved his life, Doc Bradley. Both Little Dove and Walking Bear were very interested in Earl's story about Doc saving his life. Walking Bear had to return to work and Earl and I had to return to camp.

Little Dove gave both of us a hug and we said goodbye and left.

We had only been walking on the tracks a short distance when we heard a train whistle behind us so we looked for a spot to get off the track. Shortly, a large steam engine pulling nine cars, mostly passenger cars, came roaring by, puffing steam and smoke. The cars clattered as their wheels hit each joint of the tracks. There was considerable noise and in a short time the train disappeared around a bend and the sound also disappeared. In about five minutes, we heard its whistle as it approached a crossing near Spooner.

We resumed walking back to camp and both of us remarked about the tall white pine growing on either side of the tracks as the tracks veered to the west away from the dirt road that crossed the Beaver Brook stream. I told Earl that in the heyday of the railroad in Spooner, over twenty trains a day came through town. There is a round house with a turn table where engines are turned around, or repaired.

We walked north and we could see some of the buildings up on the hill to the west of the tracks. "Who lives there?" Earl asked. "I don't know, but I did see a girl, a little older than me, come out and drive the cows up to the barn one day," I replied. Earl said, "That looks like a wonderful place to live with this great wildlife area nearby. A person would have plenty of space to fish, hunt and raise kids."

By late afternoon, we rigged up our fly rods and went to catch trout for supper. Earl was using some wet flies that

Dad brought for him and I dug up worms and fished with them. Earl went to the sluice dam hole and I went to the straight hole. Earl was to catch the trout for supper and I would only keep a trout if it was hooked badly. I caught four in the seven to nine inch range. Then I hooked a beauty. Other than one underbelly flash of white under the water, I did not see the fish for about ten minutes. This hole was long and this trout ran to the far end and back two times. I really could not hold it as I had on a three pound test leader so I really had to be gentle. The fish got tired and after about fifteen minutes, I shortened up my grip on the pole and reached my landing net. It took another two minutes before I could slip the landing net under this fighter. I carefully lifted the fish out of the water, talking to it all the time. That is silly, I know, but I felt that I owed it to the fish since I bested it in this battle.

I moved to the shore and carefully picked up the tired trout behind its gills. I removed the number 6 snelled hook with my needle nosed pliers and held it up to my measuring mark on my fly rod - twenty-one inches long! The first trout I actually caught over twenty inches. I guessed its weight at three and one-half to four pounds. This fish was a German Brown trout and it was beautiful. I carefully put this big trout back in the water and held it upright and gently released my grip. The fish moved its gills and slowly began to move its fins. It very slowly returned to the deep water. I had a warm, wonderful feeling for having caught this large fish, but most of the warmth came from letting it go back to the water. Maybe I don't have any killer instinct as I doubt if I could shoot that beautiful 10 point buck I saw earlier. I think I am beginning to realize that the trout and the buck are animals that have a life, just like I have a life. Granted their life is different from mine, but maybe not too much. Anyway, I really felt good about catching and holding the trout in my hand but letting it go was the best.

Earl really sang the praises for his new fly rod as he caught several trout but only kept a ten and one-half inch and an eleven inch one. We started a fire to cook the trout but had enough boiled water for the time being. Before we left Casey's cabin, Savannah and I set the time to fish the three spring ponds east of Beaver Brook. Elon agreed to drop Savannah off by the bridge on July 9th at 9:00 a.m. I really am looking forward to the fishing, but seeing Savannah is way better. I can't seem to get her out of my thoughts. It took over an hour to write today's story. Good night.

**July 7, 1948 - Early.**

Back to Cheerios and condensed milk for breakfast. It feels like a rainy day. We definitely could use rain - maybe today. I can hear crows putting up a big ruckus about a quarter mile away - must have found an owl or hawk to harass.

**July 7, 1948 - Late.**

By mid-morning, it began raining hard. Earl and I retreated to our tents and slept. I woke up about noon and it was still raining. Even if it stopped raining, the woods, underbrush, grass, etc. will be wet. Not much fun wading through wet brush.

I wonder what I will do when I am grown up. I probably will be drafted into the military. I hope the world will be peaceful. I don't think I want to work on the railroad like my dad. I really want to see the world. Places I have read about sound exciting. I like building and fixing things so maybe a carpenter. I could build things, like a house and say, "I built that." Maybe I could be on the city council. I was elected to the Student Council and I liked that. I know that education is very important and getting good grades is really important. Maybe I could get a scholarship to attend a big school like the University of Wisconsin. I hope to visit Madison in the next year or two. Maybe take in the Capitol on the same trip. I know that the sky is the limit, at least that is what Mom and Dad say.

The storm passed and the full moon rose in the eastern sky. Looking through the pine branches at the moon was a humbling sight. Earl and I decide to follow the trail up to the tracks because the moonlight makes it seem like day. We reach the tracks and Earl lights up a cigarette. In the distance we can hear a train whistle. In a few minutes we can hear the train coming. It is a steamer. We step back from the tracks  and soon we see the powerful light on the engine as it comes into view south of the trestle. It is headed toward Spooner and is moving quite fast. The engine passes and we can see the engineer.

It is a passenger train with ten cars counting the caboose. The cars are lit up and we can see many passengers sitting in the seats. We both wonder who is on that train. Where are they going? Why are they going?   This train could be the one called 'the fishermen special' It comes out of Chicago and targets fishermen with stops along the way, but the main stop is at Spooner. Resort owners meet the train and pick up fishermen and take them to their resorts.

This same train picks up deer hunters for the deer season in November.

Anyway, the train rapidly passes and continues north toward Spooner. In a short time it disappears and so do the sounds of the train. In a minute or two, the engineer blows the whistle for the next crossing.

Earl and I decide to go sit on the rails and enjoy the night. We talked about the two days at the Casey's cabin. We really enjoyed all the people, including John's kids. I said it was nice to be able to wash up with warm water and it was really nice to use a bathroom instead of the slit trench at camp. Earl said he was feeling much better about himself and was very happy to be accepted by me, my parents, the Casey's and John's family.

He felt very welcome, more so than anytime since he got out of the hospital. After about an hour, we heard another train coming, this time from the north. In a few minutes we saw its powerful light as it approached us. This was a diesel engine and it was pulling ten cars including the caboose. This was also a passenger train and we could see the people sitting in the lighted cars. Earl said, "I was on that train when I joined the Marines. We went through Spooner about this time on the way to Chicago from Superior. Who knows, there may be other young men and women on their way to boot camp riding in that train at this very moment."

After the train passed and signaled for the crossing at the cranberry marsh, we decided to return to camp. I told Earl that Elon was going to drop Savannah off at the bridge about 9:00 a.m. on Thursday and we were going to fish upstream from the bridge.

We just returned to camp, when all of a sudden, we heard a wild cat scream. It was not very far from us. That made the hair on the back of my neck stand up! I am pretty sure there is nothing to be afraid of, but - - - that scream was scary. Good night.

## July 8, 1948 - Early.

Earl was up before me and he spotted a doe and two fawns by the stream. He woke me so I could see them. The fawns decided they wanted to suck, so they did - both at once - their tails wagging like crazy. The fawns still had spots on their coats.

Earl said he was going to walk into Spooner today just to look around. I decided that today would be a good day to go to the sandbanks and fish. I would have to go through the meadows to get there.

## July 8, 1948 - Late.

Earl walked to Spooner, ate lunch at the 'Beanery' in the railroad depot. He went into several stores on Main Street. He got a cup of coffee at one of the restaurants and visited with a couple men there and had an enjoyable visit. He seemed very happy with his day.

I took my spinning gear, walked through the meadows and got to the sandbanks. I got in the stream and fished upstream, casting the French spinner and retrieving it downstream. I caught several trout from eight to thirteen inches, about half were German Brown trout and the others were brook trout. The stream is bigger and deeper by the sandbanks. I had to get out in three places because the water was deeper than my hip boots. Eventually, I fished my way to the meadows and found the north meadow hole. I watched for a few minutes and then made a sidearm cast toward a spot where the hole was deeper. I retrieved the spinner and got a very hard hit.

The fish stayed deep and went to my left. I really could not hold it, but it stopped and slowly swam back to my right. I was able to bring it toward me but, all at once, it came up out of the water about twelve feet from me. It appeared to be about fifteen or sixteen inches long. The fish swam right past me, headed down stream, and I was able to turn it. It took about eight minutes but I finally was able to slip the net under this beauty and lift it out of the water. I measured it at fifteen and one-half inches. I carefully removed the spinner hook and put it back in the water. It just lay there for a few seconds, but then it swam away. I was done fishing and headed for camp. Good night.

### July 9, 1948 - Early.

I had Cheerios and condensed milk for breakfast. Earl was going to visit the trestle and maybe go up on the hill by the farm to see what the view is like. I gathered up my spinning gear and headed for the bridge to meet Savannah.

### July 9, 1948 - Late.

Savannah was right on time. Elon said he would be back to pick up Savannah by 2:00 p.m. Savannah led the way and in a few minutes we came to the first pool. It was about forty feet long, twenty-five feet wide with brush growing around most of it. There was an opening and Savannah asked, "Can you do a slingshot cast?" I laughed, "Not that I know of." She showed me how to hold the rod in my right hand above the handle with the line under one finger. Next pinch the bottom of the treble hook in my left hand and give a little slack in the line, but then pull the spinner down and put a bend in the pole. She said, "Aim at the spot you want the spinner to go and let go of the spinner and the line. I will show you." She crept toward the only opening in the brush, knelt down and pulled the spinner down, putting a big bend in the pole, and let it go. Presto! The line flew out in the middle of the pool. Savannah retrieved it and got a strike. She was able to reel in the trout and it was about nine inches. She returned it to the pool.

It was my turn and I gave it a try. I surprised myself as the spinner shot out to the middle of the pool. I did not catch anything, but just as I was about to lift the lure out of the water, a good sized fish, a trout I think, tried to bite the spinner. It missed but scared me plenty. Savannah tried another sling shot and the same thing happened to her. She told me, "Take a crack at it but this time make a figure eight with your lure before you lift it out of the water." I shot the spinner out into the pool and barely started retrieving it when I got a strong hit on the lure. I could hardly hold the fish and it went under the overhanging brush on the east side of the pool. My line went into the bushes and I figured it would get tangled and the fish would get off. In a few seconds, the fish headed toward the west side of the pool and my line came free. After about two more minutes, I was able to bring the fish toward me and Savannah put the net under it. We carefully removed the spinner and measured it. It was fifteen and one-half inches long and it was a brook trout. We carefully returned this beauty back to the pool.

Savannah said we needed to go to the middle pool, so we followed the small stream to the northeast and after about seventy-five yards there was the spring pond. It was about seventy-five feet in diameter with bushes growing around most of it but there were two or three openings where we might be able to make an overhead cast. We stayed low and crept into these openings about twenty-five feet apart. We started casting and caught trout with just about every cast. The largest was fourteen inches and all were returned to the pool.

We continued northeast and after about one hundred yards we came to the third pool. This was the nicest of the three pools. There were very few bushes, but there were cattails and lily pads in two places. The pond was about seventy five feet across and was surrounded by trees, mostly oaks, maple and ash. Wow, it was a beautiful spot.

Before we could start fishing, Savannah said she thought she had a wood tick crawling on her back. She asked me to help her get it off her back. I said I would, so Savannah took off her creel, her fishing coat and then her blouse! She was facing away from me but it still was quite a sight. She said it felt like it was under her bra strap and could I look under it and see if it was there. I said I would and carefully rolled the bra strap and, sure enough, there was the wood tick which I grabbed and told her I got it. With that she turned around to see it and I saw her! "Whoops," she said and turned away and put her blouse back on. My face must have been beet red! Thinking about this as I write - it was quite the sight for a young boy to see!

Savannah finished getting her fishing gear on and apologized for not being more modest. Anyway, we sized up this wonderful pool and started casting those spinners. We caught trout with nearly every cast. All were released but then Savannah got a hard hit. I could tell it was a large fish as Savannah could not hold it and the drag on her reel was clicking. Fortunately, it was a small pool so the runs this fish made were short. For twenty minutes we did not see this big trout. Finally, Savannah was able to slowly move it toward her, a few inches at a time. I got the net ready but as I was reaching to put the net under the fish, it made one last desperate thrash - water flew everywhere - and this beauty managed to get free. It slowly swam away and in a few seconds it disappeared in the depths.

Savannah was smiling. She did a good job of fighting this fish and she said, "I admire the fish for giving it all it had to escape. Too bad it didn't know we were going to release it anyway. Wow! That was some fish. Let's head to the bridge."

On the way back to the bridge, we stopped once and Savannah asked, "Did you have a strange feeling when you saw me partly dressed? I know I did." I stammered and looked down. "I certainly did have a strange, but wonderful feeling sweep over me. I think it is still affecting me but we better continue on." Savannah said, "I know we are close to the bridge and I may not see you for awhile. I have church camp next week and then we go to Antigo for a few days. I should be back by July 23rd. I will try to get Dad to bring me to the stream and I will find you. For now, I want to give you a kiss." She pulled me to her and we kissed, a real nice kiss. One that further messed up my feelings toward Savannah. I am beginning to think of her as a special friend - maybe real special. She sure is good looking with that red hair and maybe she is sexy. I am beginning to think of her as more than a trout fishing girl, even though she is really good at catching trout. I wonder what love is. Good night.

## July 10, 1948 - Early.

I didn't see Earl last night. At breakfast he told of going to the trestle, into the pasture where he saw a man and a boy riding on a Ford tractor. They crossed the stream and went up near the tracks and appeared to be working on the fence. He saw the cows and they did not come after him. He went up by the barn on the hill and looked out over this valley. He was impressed. In the field north of the hill farm, a family was putting up hay. They had a tractor that pulled a hay wagon with a machine that picked up hay and brought it up onto the wagon. Two people with forks arranged it on the wagon. Earl said, "I could see one of the people was a kid and was struggling to keep up. I walked out of the woods and volunteered my help and the Dad accepted. I helped put up hay all afternoon and after that I helped with the milking. The farm buildings are across the highway. I did not get home until after dark, but I had a great day." As I was writing this I heard something hit the tarp and roll off and it landed a couple of feet from me. It was an owl pellet. This pellet was from one of the saw-whet owls in the big pines in camp. We had owl pellets in science class last year.

## July 10, 1948 - Late.

I laid around camp, cut some firewood, but did not do much. I met Dad's train in late afternoon. Mom sent Cheerios, Spam, cookies, condensed milk, small red potatoes, clean clothes and a short letter. Earl was very talkative and told me about growing up in Superior. He had two friends that fished in the St. Louis River. In the fall they hunted ducks there also. He told about hunting on Armistice Day about 1940. The day was warm and pleasant, but a violent, cold storm blew in. High winds, snow and bitter cold temperatures. Earl and his buddies picked up their decoys and were able to get home safely but dozens of duck hunters froze to death that day. Most of them were around the Mississippi River between Wisconsin and Minnesota. Earl trapped muskrats and one fall he caught over one hundred but it was hard to do that and go to school.

He told about deer hunting with his dad on some property near Solon Springs, Wisconsin. There was a logging trail going through the property and Earl and his dad were quietly walking with fresh snow on the ground. The trail split and Earl's dad took the left fork. Earl had gone about one hundred yards when a big buck jumped up out of his bed and ran across the logging road at about sixty-five yards from Earl. He was ready for it to cross the road even though it was running flat out. Earl shot and hit the buck in the neck and it went down immediately. It was an eleven pointer and weighed 186 pounds. Earl said, "That was the biggest thrill I ever got hunting. Just seeing that beautiful buck was great and being able to shoot it was a big thrill for me." Good night.

**July 11, 1948 - Early.**

Two chickadees flitted around the camp this morning. A chipmunk visited camp, apparently looking for anything to eat. This is the first 'chippy' I have seen in camp. We decide that we need more firewood so we will work on that today. By now we have used up all the dry wood near camp so it means having to carry it one to two hundred yards. That will give us a good workout.

**July 11, 1948 - Late.**

By late afternoon, Earl wanted to catch enough trout for supper so he took his fishing gear and headed to the beaver pond. In an hour, he returned with four trout, all eight and one-half to eleven inches long. We got a fire going and boiled water and then fried the trout along with some of the new red potatoes Mom had sent. We also had fresh bread and cookies. I saw a doe and two fawns down by the stream. Good night.

**July 12, 1948 - Early.**

Earl will walk to Spooner. He needs to buy cigarettes. I will take the path from the beaver pond up the hill toward the house on the gravel road.

**July 12, 1948 - Late.**

I followed the path and saw the house. Could hear kids playing. Got on the gravel road and walked south to the bridge over Beaver Brook. The road drops down to the bridge as it goes south and rises again after crossing the bridge. There are some very large white pines on both sides of the road and it is quite beautiful. I sat on a large rock by the stream and almost under the bridge. After about ten minutes, I saw a nice trout in the sixteen inch range under the bridge. About one hundred yards south of the bridge is a beautiful stand of large white pine. I guess that there are about a hundred trees from small diameter to large ones, two to three feet in diameter. I wander in this majestic grove and admired how tall and straight these trees are. They are in the Beaver Brook Wildlife Area.

I decided to return to camp by walking between the stream and the railroad tracks. I had never explored this area except for the woods around the trestle. There was no trail, but lots of great scenery as there are many large white pines growing near the stream. The banks in some places are very steep and up to fifty feet high. I could look down on the stream in several locations and I was impressed by the beauty I was seeing.

Eventually, I came to the edge of a spruce swamp. It was not large, maybe an acre or two, and on the north side of it was a fence which I crossed. This must be where cows from the hilltop came under the trestle and could eat grass, leaves, etc. As I walked north, I came to the small stream that flows under the roots in many places. There are many large trees here too, and looking toward the trestle, which is slightly uphill and toward the west, is about as pretty a sight as I have ever seen. I sat by the pool that the ten point buck came and drank out of and saw several small trout zipping around but no big buck showed up.

The den for the three red fox pups was on my way back to camp so I found it and, as I approached, I saw one pup run into the den. I sat down about fifteen feet away and watched to see if it would come out. After about ten minutes, a pup came out and immediately saw me but it came out of the den anyway. Right behind it came the other two and all three proceeded to sit and watch me. After about five minutes, I started talking to them. They would turn their head as if they were trying to figure out the words. After about ten minutes one pup stood up and walked in my direction. After another five minutes it was within three feet of me and I slowly put out my hand. The pup stretched its nose out and sniffed, took a step and started licking my hand! By now the other two had joined the first pup and they would not lick my hand, but smelled it. After a few minutes, they heard something toward the west and they all took off and were out of sight in a flash.

As I sat watching the three fox pups, I remembered hearing a squawking sound west of the camp. It was about two hours after sunset in late June and the squawking continued for several minutes but it was moving from south to north. I took the flashlight and my gun and went to investigate this strange sound. I have to admit that I was a little scared - but I went looking for whatever was making this strange sound and only about seventy five to one hundred yards away. I had a strange flow of emotions! I was scared! Is whatever making this sound dangerous? Is this some animal new to this area? Is this sound maker to be feared?

Why am I going looking for this critter in the dark of the night, with a puny flashlight which might fail and leave me completely in the dark, and at the mercy of this strange, and apparently dangerous, animal. Anyway, knees knocking, I proceeded up the trail towards the railroad tracks. All at once, this dangerous animal, with its hideous scream stepped out on the trail about twenty-five yards away and let out one of its horrid screams. It was a fox! Whew!! Talk about a let down. For whatever reason I had not written about this event in my diary, but now I have and my knees have stopped knocking.

## July 13, 1948 - Early.

It was cold last night. I put on all my blankets and I was still cold. Could it be cold enough to cause the cranberry marsh to flood the berries? After breakfast, I decided to hike the tracks for one and one-half miles to see if the cranberry bogs are flooded and they were! I stopped at Little Dove's shack and asked if she would call the folks at Birchwood and tell them about the anticipated release of extra water down Beaver Brook. She said she would, but wanted me to stay and have some breakfast as Walking Bear was working at the marsh. I told her I had already eaten but thanks anyway. Little Dove definitely didn't want me to leave. She is very nice, pretty actually, but I knew I had to say, "Good-bye and thank you for calling." I told her that we would give them some nice trout - hopefully.

I was happy to leave Little Dove, but I easily could have stayed. She is very pleasant, quite curvy, very much like Savannah. I sure miss Savannah. I am afraid Savannah and her parents are at church camp and will miss this possibility to catch some very nice trout. Maybe Margaret Burns will be able to return to Beaver Brook and catch some nice trout. I don't think she met Earl when we were at the Casey cabin last week. Maybe they will meet on the stream. Whoa! Both are single - maybe.

I returned to camp and found Earl digging worms. He had gotten all his fishing gear prepared, dug plenty of worms and was ready. He planned to wait by the big pine hole and work downstream from there. He knew that many other people could be fishing and he certainly would be happy to share the best  holes. I didn't know if there would be a flood down the stream or when it would happen. All I know is that I plan to be ready, if and when it happens. I have been camping, fishing and exploring for one and one-half months now.

## July 13, 1948 - Late.

The big flood finally happened! The slow moving wall of water got to camp just after noon. It was really something to see. A wall of water about one foot high, flushing anything on the banks into the water. I picked up my gear and headed for the sluice dam hole. I beat the wall of water there so I waited. Here it comes! I knew where a big trout had been but during this brief flood, the trout apparently come out and gobble up any food that is in the water - a real feeding frenzy.

I floated a worm on a number 6 hook and split shot and before it had gone fifteen feet I saw a large fish swirl near the bait and in an instant I felt a fish on my line. I set the hook  and immediately realized that this fast moving extra water made playing the fish much harder. This big fish got off the line. I moved down stream to the meadow curve which under normal water is under the bank. Today the water is even with the bank. I float the worm near the bank and bang! There is a hard hit. I set the hook and struggle to keep the trout from going downstream. After about ten minutes, I netted this beauty and it is seventeen inches long. This one is for Little Dove and Walking Bear, so in the creel it goes, along with some fresh grass.

I really had my eye on the north meadow hole as I knew there should be a four or five pound trout there, but the undercut hole is upstream from it. The water is so high I must fish from shore and I float a worm in the undercut hole and catch a fat eleven and one-half inch brown trout.

I am nervous about the north meadow hole so I continue towards it. The stream is naturally larger here and today it is very high. Just upstream from the hole are some slight rapids and I use a stick to see how deep the water is. My hip boots were able to keep me dry as I moved out into the stream.

I decided to put an extra split shot on my leader and I put three worms on the number 6 hook. I thought that normally the big trout was in a deep hole on the east side of this beautiful hole. I floated the worm into that deep hole and nothing happened. I withdrew the worm and tried a little to the west. Nothing. I withdrew and took off one split shot down to two. I tried the deep hole again and I felt a fish on the line. I took the slack up and set the hook. It felt like I snagged a log as nothing moved. I set the hook again and wow. All at once a very large trout jumped out of the water. That was my fish and it must be four or five pounds. I really doubted I had the skill, or the equipment, to land this beauty, but we were into it now. This fish ran downstream and I could not stop it until it pulled out all of my fly line and nearly all the back up line. Finally, it stopped, around the next bend.

Now I had a problem. The water was too deep for me to

follow unless I just waded in over my hip boots. That is what I did. I was able to take up some line as the big fish seemed to be staying in one spot. I took my billfold out of my pants and put it under my cap and slowly made my way toward the fish. All at once, it was on the move going further downstream. I followed trying to keep tension on the fish. I had to duck under two groups of tag alder that reached out over the stream. By now we had gone about a hundred yards downstream, but I was able to move the fish - a little. Finally, I could walk near the fish and I tried to lift it off the bottom. It came a little, but then ran back up stream. I slogged along after it and was able to get it to the surface once for about two seconds and then it went to the bottom. Eventually, I was able to get this beauty into the net. I measured it at twenty and one-half inches. I guessed it to weigh four to five pounds. I carefully removed the hook and returned this huge German brown trout back into its hole and in a few seconds it slowly swam deep into the water and disappeared. That was a wonderful fish but I was proud of my performance, too.

I broke down my fly rod and headed for camp with my wet hip boots. By the time I went by the sluice dam hole the water level looked like it was about normal. When I got to camp, Earl was there but so was Margaret Burns. They had met at the big pine tree hole and fished together down to camp. They had great luck and between their creels, they had two - eleven inches and one - thirteen inch, two - fourteen inches and one - seventeen inch. We decided to give a seventeen inch and a fourteen inch trout to Little Dove and Walking Bear.

It turned out that the Casey's and Savannah were not

home so they missed out on this event. Margaret hoped we would fry some trout for supper, so she brought a few potatoes out of her garden. We got a fire going and fried the trout and potatoes and had a great supper, at least by my standards. We had cookies for dessert.

After supper, Earl told me he was going to leave with Margaret and he was going to put new shingles on her house. He would be staying with her in her house so he would be taking his tent and all of his gear with him when he and Margaret headed to her car. Apparently, Margaret and Earl got to be good friends as they fished together. Perhaps they had met when we spent time with the Casey's around the 4th of July.

By early evening, Margaret and Earl left camp and I was left wondering how things would work out for the two of them. Margaret appeared to be a few years older than Earl but she did seem like a very caring person and would be good for Earl.

Before supper, Earl said he had given a great amount of thought to possibly visiting Doc Bradley at Antigo. Even though he really admired Doc, Earl was worried that seeing Doc may bring back all the terrible memories that he was struggling with. He had talked to Margaret about Doc as well as his memories of Iwo Jima and she felt he probably should not look up Doc and supported Earl's decision not to. Earl gave me a hug before he and Margaret left camp. He thanked me for being a good friend and he felt my friendship helped him deal with his war time problems. He promised to keep in touch as he had my folks address in Spooner plus their phone number.

I had come to really admire and like Earl. We were good friends even though he was about ten years older than I was. Somehow, we both were good for each other. As we shook hands as Earl and Margaret were about to leave, he said, "I will miss this camp. It is a special place." I could see Earl was close to having a tear or two, but he picked up his gear and along with Margaret, headed to the car by the bridge. I wonder if I will ever see Earl again. Maybe the two of them will get married. Anyway, I am alone in camp, but I will miss Earl.

## July 14, 1948 - Early.

I heard howling off in the distance during the night. I sure wonder what that is. Timber wolves are very scarce in Wisconsin at this time. I guess it could be timber wolves. Whatever it is, I hope it stays far away.

## July 14, 1948 - Late.

I went to the sluice dam and tried to picture what went on there. The four 12" x 12" timbers that go across the stream make up the base of the dam. I can see where dirt was dug out on both ends of the timbers. There is a natural ridge that the stream cuts through so if someone was making a dam, there already is a large part of it here. The stream channel cut through this ridge possibly shortly after the glaciers melted. Dad said that these sluice dams were located where a large amount of water could be dammed up in a valley, slough or a swamp lowland. The dam was built during the summer or fall but during the late winter somehow the dam was closed. When the spring melt occurred the dam would hold back water so it could be released to produce a flood that the lumberjacks could roll the pine logs into and the logs would float downstream to the mill to be sawed into lumber. Dad thought that this dam was built about 1900 A.D.

I sat down and tried to picture the men working that built this dam about fifty years ago. First thing is - where did these huge timbers come from and how did they get to the stream and put in place. By walking on the beams I figured they were eighteen feet long. That is what was not buried in the bank. These timbers were 12" x 12" and must have been twenty-two feet long, at least, and maybe longer. All four beams are on the same level and are about four feet apart. I could find no nails or bolts on the beams. There are no holes bored into these beams. Apparently they are the base for the dam, but all the water in Beaver Brook runs under these beams. I have an idea what a sluice dam may look like as I saw pictures of two of them in a book at the library in school.

I wonder where these huge beams came from and how did they get hauled here and put in place. My guess is that the lumber company that had the contract to cut the timber on the land around here, sawed the timbers and they were hauled by teams of horses or oxen, through the woods from the northeast to a spot up east of the dam. They were unloaded and the horses or oxen pulled them near the site for the dam. My guess is that a crew had prepared both sides of the stream for the timbers. A horse could pull one of the timbers to a spot near the stream. Maybe the horse could be led across the stream and a long chain or cable used to pull the beams into place. Earlier we found a wagon road that could have been the route these beams got to the stream.

There should have been way more to this sluice dam than these four timbers. I searched both sides of the stream down stream for at least a quarter of a mile. I have fished in the stream for that same distance and have never found any evidence of other dam making material like boards, timbers or other evidence of material.

Another thought crossed my mind. Maybe these four beams are as far as the dam got built or maybe the lumber company went bankrupt or worked a deal with the railroad to put in a spur and haul the logs to the mill. The sluice dam site is only about one third of a mile from the railroad tracks that were built about 1879.

As I sat thinking about this dam, it occurred to me that the beaver pond could have been a huge back up of water. The beaver pond is held back by a large beaver dam now and may have been like that when the sluice dam was being built. A couple of sticks of dynamite would have blown a good sized hole in the dam and this water could have aided the floating of logs down to the mill. The beaver pond is about one hundred twenty-five yards up stream from the sluice dam.

I see where soil was dug out of the ridges on either side of the four timbers. What was the dirt used for? There was a significant amount of dirt moved and I wonder where it was moved to. Apparently it must have been part of the dam, if there was one. Maybe planks were used to form the dam and the dirt may have been added to give the dam more strength once the snow began to melt.

I can picture all of the workers doing their assigned jobs as the dam took shape, if it was built. I can picture a four to five acre pond with water five to six feet deep behind the sluice dam. Pine logs had been cut all winter and were stacked in several locations, on either side of Beaver Brook below the dam. If it was a normal winter, by the end of March most of the snow would have melted and the pond behind the dam was as full as it would get. Workers would have gotten rid of any obstacles below the dam so once the logs are rolled into the water, hopefully they will not get hung up and make a log jam. Lumberjacks with long pike poles will be stationed at places that could cause jams. Finally, the dam is opened and a huge flood of water flows down stream. Lumberjacks roll pine logs into this flood and off they go. Hopefully all the logs will make their way to the mill during this flood. I can see that if a jam occurs and the logs get stuck, the flood water will pass and when the jam is cleared there may not be enough water to float the logs to the mill. Now what?

Whatever happened, I can only guess at. What I am sure of is that there are four 12" x 12" timbers that span Beaver Brook at a point where a dam could have been built. I have no evidence of anything else except places where dirt was dug out of the ridge. All of this must have taken place about fifty or more years ago.

**July 15, 1948 - Early.**

Right after I got up, I heard something rustling near the wood pile. All at once, in a few seconds it disappeared, but reappeared about three feet away. It looked at me for a few seconds and then it was gone. Shortly, it poked its head out at a different place. In a few seconds it was gone. This went on for several minutes so I went over near the wood pile. That was too much for this little critter and away it ran. It was long and skinny - a weasel! It had a jumping sort of gait as it ran. It seems strange but badgers and wolverines are members of the weasel family, but so are skunks and otters! Wow!

**July 17, 1948 - Early.**

This should be Savannah's last day at church camp. I hope she can come and see me tomorrow. I will keep looking for her and will wait by the big pine hole. I need to meet Dad's train this afternoon. I feel like just lying around camp today.

**July 18, 1948 - Early.**

Had to visit the slit trench during the night and, as I walked there, something flew past me and before I could get the flashlight around it was gone. As I looked for it, all of a sudden, something flew through my flashlight beam. I saw that it was a flying squirrel! The other thing must have been one also. This one landed on the base of one of the large white pines in camp. These small squirrels have extra skin between their front and hind legs which, when they spread their legs, this extra skin acts like a glider and the squirrel can glide from a high place to a lower place. They are out at night so most people never see them. In a few seconds, two more flyers sailed through my flashlight beam. A family of flyers!! I will go to the big pine and wait for Savannah.

**July 18, 1948 - Late.**

Savannah did come! We fished a little and she told me

about church camp. She really enjoyed camp and she could get together with friends she has met before. Sounds like a lot of fun. When we were about one hundred fifty yards from camp, a thunderstorm appeared all of a sudden. The rain came down in buckets and we got drenched. We ran to camp but we were soaked to the skin. Luckily, it was warm.

We got under the tarp and took off our fishing gear. We went into my tent and sat on the cot. We were both shivering so we decided to take off our shirts. I found dry shirts to put on but I grabbed a blanket to put around us first. Wow! Savannah just had her bra on and I was looking. We sat on the cot with the blanket around us when Savannah said she had to take off her wet bra.

I put my arm around Savannah's shoulder to hold the blanket in place. We sat like this for a few minutes and we kissed several times. Then Savannah pushed me down on the cot and she put the blanket over both of us. She laid down beside me! Super WOW! What a wonderful feeling to feel her warm body - the warmth felt great. She really has pretty eyes.

We laid under the blanket for about half an hour. Nothing more happened. I know I thought we had gone a long, long way today and I was too scared to do anything else, whatever it might be. Savannah seemed to feel about the same way so eventually we sheepishly got out from under the blanket, put on dry shirts and hunted up some lunch. By this time, it was mid-afternoon and Savannah had to meet her folks at the bridge by four o'clock.

Savannah and I crossed the stream and headed to the

bridge to meet her parents. We did not talk much but held hands whenever we could. We talked about Savannah going to Antigo with her parents on Monday. Both of us felt the summer was winding down. We talked more as we walked closer to the bridge. She knew that Earl was living at Margaret Burns place and was going to replace the shingles. She thought there might be more going on than that and hoped the two of them could be happy and maybe get married. Margaret had hinted to Savannah's mom that 'she liked what she saw'.

I had already thought about the few days left at the camp. I needed to get the dates but I wanted to be home for the county fair which I thought was the first part of August. Also, I was going to go out for football and maybe this weekend, when Mom and Dad visit, I will know when I need to report.

Savannah also was checking the calendar and she also realized that our wonderful summer was winding down. Savannah had it figured that the end of the next week and one-half would be the end of our summer together. Since we could not communicate, we needed to plan ahead and hope our plans work out.

Just before we reached the bridge, Savannah stopped and pulled me to her and said, "Wouldn't it be great if all the people that you and I know and met this summer could get together for a picnic!" That idea caught me by complete surprise, but after a few seconds, I said, "Yes, that would be great."

"What did you have in mind?" I asked. Savannah said, "How about everyone meeting at Little Dove and Walking

Bear's place?" This girl is a thinker. I said, "It sounds like a fun time. When would we try to do it?" Savannah said, "How about a week from today, at noon. We could have a potluck dinner." With that, we lock in a long embrace and had a long emotional kiss.

When Savannah's folks arrived, Savannah asked them what they thought of the idea of a pot luck picnic at Little Dove and Walking Bear's place a week from today. That met with a positive response and felt we should go for it but we need to get approval from Little Dove and Walking Bear. I said I would talk to them and to my mom and dad tomorrow. Savannah would talk to Margaret and Earl.

I made my way back to camp. My mind was on Savannah and I don't remember much about my return to camp. That girl is real special and she is in my thoughts constantly. I don't know if this is love, but - maybe it is.

## July 19, 1948 - Early.

I heard a loud screech, coming from the white pines in camp. I heard it again and I could not identify it. I decided to walk toward the south to see if I could see what was making all this noise. I guessed it was a bird. A large bird, from the volume of the screech.

I carefully walked south, looking up in to the large pine trees. When I was about 150 feet away from camp I could see the screech maker. It was a bald eagle! The very first one I had ever seen. It was impressive as it sat on a high limb and looked at me. We watched each other for at least fifteen minutes and then it spread its huge wings, dipped forward and down, then took off. It gave one final screech as it left. Wow! A bald eagle. Mom and Dad are coming at noon. I am really looking forward to seeing them and asking them to come to the picnic next Saturday.

## July 19, 1948 - Late.

Mom brought that great fried chicken for dinner. She also brought potatoes, cucumbers, cookies, bread and clean clothes. We talked about my summer winding down and they liked the idea of the potluck picnic next Saturday. They would be happy to come and Mom said she would bring fried chicken and other things. Dad said he would bring some cokes and cream soda to drink.

The Spooner paper Mom and Dad brought confirmed that the Washburn County Fair was the $6^{th}$, $7^{th}$ and $8^{th}$ of August. Football practice started with gear being picked up on Saturday, August $8^{th}$ at 9:00 a.m. for varsity and 10:00 a.m. for freshman. Practice begins at 9:00 a.m. on Monday, August $10^{th}$.

That pretty well formed my schedule. I needed to break camp by Saturday, August $1^{st}$ and Sunday, August $2^{nd}$. That is if it is alright with Mom and Dad, especially Dad, since he would need to help me pack things from camp out to the car and then home. Home. I have thought about it more lately. My summer in the woods has been wonderful, but I am feeling urges to return home and get ready to be a freshman in high school. It scares me some, but I am ready for whatever challenges I may face, I hope. I really hate to think that I won't see Savannah much anymore. In fact, I may not see her ever again! That would be terrible. We both plan to write letters, but Antigo is a long way from Spooner and since neither of us are old enough to drive, we would have to rely on others, probably our moms and dads, to drive us to see each other. We will just have to wait and see how things work out. I imagine that I will see Ellen, maybe at the fair, and who knows what will come of that, if anything.

As I write this, I hear two large animals howling, not far away. Maybe they are by the beaver pond. It is dark. I get my rifle in readiness, right by my cot. This is the first time all summer I have been afraid. I checked the closing on the tent flap and they are OK. I am going to turn off my light and crawl in bed. I sure hope I can get to sleep.

## July 20, 1948 - Early.

My birthday is today! I slept like a log. I did not hear any more howling and no strange sounds. As I was eating breakfast I was aware of a large object flying just to my right. It was an owl. It landed on the lower limb of an elm tree on the other side of the stream. I could see its horns. It was a great horned owl. Dad and I saw one last year about one mile north of camp. It had just settled in when, all at once, three more great horned owls flew into that same elm tree. What a sight. A family of owls. Maybe these owls will stay in this area and maybe they will talk to each other. I no sooner wrote this when one owl let out whoo-whoo-hoo-hoo! Or something like that. What a beautiful sound and sight. Today Savannah and her folks go to Antigo for three or four days.

**July 20, 1948 - Late.**

This evening I went to get some water out of the stream to boil for drinking. On a small sand bar, just below the camp, I saw huge dog type tracks! They are about four or more inches in diameter. They must have been made by a timber wolf! That wolf was only a few feet from my tent with me in it. Now that is scary. I will carry my .22 rifle with me until I feel better about this wolf thing.

**July 21, 1948 - Early.**

During the night I heard several owls hooting back and forth. This morning I could see one of the great horned owls sitting in the same elm tree. I did not hear any wolf howls last night but I am keeping an eye open for them.

**July 21, 1948 - Late.**

About mid-morning a man walked down the trail from the railroad tracks. He shouted hello and asked if he could come into camp. Of course he was welcome. His name was Gordon Mac. I didn't catch his last name. He worked as a sports writer for the *Superior Evening Telegram* and wanted to talk to me. That about blew me away. He said, "I was a good friend of Earl Burke and he told me about you and said I should go see you and maybe do a story about you."

This man seemed friendly, but I really did not want him to write about me. I invited him to sit down, even though I really didn't want him to pry into what I was doing this summer. I flat out told him, "NO STORY!" He said he would honor that request. He also said he wanted to talk to me and find out how I knew Earl Burke.

Gordon was a jolly, friendly guy and I liked him, but the last thing I wanted was some story about my summer in the Beaver Brook Wildlife Area. I told Gordon about meeting Earl and how he was struggling to get over what happened at Iwo Jima.

We visited for a least half an hour about Earl. It turned out Gordon was one of Earl's hunting and fishing buddies from before the war.

Gordon said Earl told him about the sluice dam and Joe Pachoes winter den. He also told Gordon about the beaver pond and several of the best trout holes on the stream. Gordon was really interested in my mom and dad and finally he asked about Savannah. About then, I clammed up and didn't say any more. Gordon kept asking about things, but I just looked at him. Finally, he asked if I would show him the sluice dam. Somehow, this didn't seem like he was prying into my life so I told him, "Let's go."

We walked to the sluice dam and Gordon was impressed by the four big timbers spanning the stream. He tried to visualize what the dam looked like and what would have taken place when the dam was opened and the pine logs rolled into the flood. He said his grandfather was a lumberjack and worked in the Spooner area for three or four years. Perhaps he worked cutting logs to be floated below the sluice dam. We spent an hour at the dam. Gordon was really fascinated by it. He also was impressed by how good the water near the dam was for trout. He told me he really liked to fish and had fished the

Brule River many times.  He really liked what he saw.

Next he asked about Joe Pachoe.  I took him through the meadows to the blow down pile that was Joe's home one winter.  I had brought the flashlight so Gordon could look around.  He also had heard the legend of Joe Pachoe but he really thought it was not true.  Finding this den doesn't prove Joe was here but like Gordon said, "Someone spent a lot of time getting this place ready for the winter."

Next he wanted to see the beaver pond, so we went back to the sluice dam and walked across the stream on one of the timbers.  Since the beaver pond is about 125 yards to the southeast, it didn't take long to get there.  Gordon was amazed at the height of the beaver dam and the beauty of the pond.  We saw several ducks and one beaver swam where we could see it.  I didn't tell Gordon anything about catching trout and releasing them.  I did tell him that I caught enough trout so I could eat trout for supper every other night.

By now it was early afternoon and Gordon said he needed to get back to Superior.  I offered to make him a peanut butter and jelly sandwich for lunch.  He said he would like that. We returned to camp and ate lunch.  After eating, I asked him where his car was parked.  He said it was south about one mile, just off the railroad tracks.  I said since you have to walk that way, let me show you a pretty sight involving a small stream.  We walked to the little stream and started toward the trestle.  Gordon stopped several times and said, "This is as beautiful a spot as I have ever seen."  I agreed and we walked up to the trestle, climbed the trestle steps and got to the railroad tracks.  Before we said good-bye, I reminded Gordon, NO STORY!  He promised that he would keep his word. He said he really enjoyed the day and I really think he was sincere. Just as we were parting, he thanked me for helping Earl heal. Gordon said, "You may have saved Earl's life."

That surprised me. Somehow, the time Earl and I spent in the camp and all the things we did, fishing, exploring and meeting other people was very important to Earl. I did see a steady improvement in Earl's outlook. He was gaining confidence and he was able to walk without much of a limp and he seemed very intelligent. When Earl left camp to go live with Margaret, I had an empty, strange feeling. I had come to really like and admire Earl. I am looking forward to seeing him at the party on Saturday.

Back to Gordon. This friendly, cordial man really seemed to enjoy his time in and around camp. Apparently he and Earl have a strong friendship that goes back to their kid days. I will have to look for Gordon's name in the *Superior Evening Telegram*. I hope he was honest with me, for sure he better not do a story about me.

### July 22, 1948 - Early.

I heard the saw-whet owl up in the big white pine on the west side of the camp. In about a minute, another saw-whet owl answered right above me. I went out from under the tarp and looked up and, sure enough, there sat three owlets on the same branch. While eating breakfast, I heard something walking steadily down near the stream. It didn't sound like a deer and I could not see any large animal. I went to investigate and here came this critter. It was a porcupine  The first one I had seen this summer. I went near it and it climbed up an elm tree. The 'porky' climbed about ten feet and stopped. It watched me but didn't climb any higher. I went back to finish breakfast and within ten minutes, the 'porky' backed down the tree. I wondered if it could cross the stream or was it destined to always be on this side. While returning to the tent, I discovered some wintergreen plants very close to the ground. These small plants have small red berries under their leaves. I ate some and they definitely tasted like wintergreen. Really good.

**July 22, 1958 - Late**

I think Savannah is coming back from Antigo today. I decided to follow the path from the beaver pond toward the house on the dirt road. I guess I was hoping to see one or two of those boys I had seen earlier. I got to the road and could see the roof of the house about a block away. I could hear kids voices but no one was visible. After a couple hours, I headed back to the beaver pond. I followed the well worn trail and when I came to the steep hill I saw a spot where a large tree had fallen and I could see the farm on the hilltop west of the railroad tracks. That must be over a mile away but I could see the barn and another building.

As I stood admiring the view, I heard voices coming from the east, or behind me. I turned and saw two boys carrying fish poles. They had seen me so I decided to see who it was. In a short time they reached me and we all said "Hi". They were Dick and Joe and they lived in the house on the dirt road. Joe looked familiar as I had seen him around school. Dick seemed about my age but I had never seen him before. They want to know about me and I told them that I had walked in from the railroad tracks.

They wanted to know if I wanted to fish with them, so I said sure and off we went.

When we got to the beaver pond, they went to the west side where the beaver dam was. They used cane poles and bobbers. They put on several worms on each hook and skillfully got the bobber and worms out in the water. In a flash, Dick's bobber went down and he pulled up a nice ten inch brook trout. They had a canvas creel between them and after adding grass to the creel they put the trout in. Joe was next and he pulled in a nice eight inch brook trout.

As they fished, we talked and Dick said he was going to be an eighth grader at the Shell Lake School. He had been going to a rural school up on Highway 70. Their family was going to move in the next week or two and their new home was on the boundary of the Spooner and Shell Lake Schools. Joe would continue going to Spooner high school as would his older sister and brother.

I spent at least an hour with Dick and Joe. I found them to be very friendly, kind and easy to talk with. They told of hunting ducks on the beaver pond. Joe said they had a 16 gauge shot gun with a 38 inch barrel and it was called 'Long Tom'. They claimed they could shoot ducks that were out of range for most shot guns. I asked about deer hunting and Dick said he shot a six point buck last season. I asked how he did it and Dick said he could see where the deer had been eating acorns under the oak trees so he found a good spot and sat down and waited. By late afternoon of the first day of season, this buck came into view. He waited until it got to a spot where he had a good shot. He raised his gun and fired. The buck went down.  About now, Dick had a big grin on his face.

I decided to leave Dick and Joe and return to camp and as I was leaving, Joe said, "I am pretty sure I saw you driving a 1937 Ford and you could not get up the big hill and had to back down. Then you had more speed and you made it up the hill.  I was in the woods to the west of the road and I know you didn't see me."

It sure sounded like Joe saw me so I said, "This lady and I were trout fishing and she got sick and I had to get her to a doctor in Spooner.  That was the first time I had ever driven a car and it was scary."

I said goodbye and hightailed it across the beaver dam and the 12" x 12" timbers.  That was close!  I got to camp and decided to just sit and listen, look and think.  I hope Savannah is back from Antigo.

### July 23, 1948 - Early.

The only visitors to camp this morning were a chipmunk and two chickadees.

### July 24, 1948 - Late.

I hung around camp yesterday hoping Savannah would come to see me.  About mid-morning, I heard a whistle across the stream and it was Savannah!  I waded across the stream and greeted Savannah with a hug and a kiss. She looked great!

Her folks dropped her off to come and ask me if I wanted to join them and Savannah and go to the Tri-State Fair at

Superior today. We all could spend the night with her dad's folks at Cable and they really wanted me to come with them. It sounded fine to me, so Savannah and I went back to my campsite to secure my things and I could change into clean clothes. We then followed the stream back to the bridge where Elon and Kathy were waiting. Off we went to Superior. I had never been to the Tri-State Fair before but I had heard about it.

We had a blast. We all rode on many of the rides like the Tilt-A-Whirl, the Trabent, Ferris Wheel and Rollo plane. The trabent was the most fun for me. We threw baseballs, shot BB guns and tossed wooden rings at bottles. Elon and Kathy paid for everything and we all had a wonderful time. We checked out the exhibits of cattle, sheep, pigs and chickens. Finally, by late afternoon, we headed toward Cable and Savannah's grandparents home.

Cable is a small town of only a few hundred people in northwest Wisconsin. Their library is in a log building but the town seemed very nice and there were a lot of people around. Savannah's grandparents lived just out of town, right on the banks of the Namekagon River. They are retired now but her grandmother was an elementary teacher in Cable and her grandfather had worked for many years at a lumber company in Drummond, a few miles away. Both folks were very friendly and made me feel at home. Apparently Elon or Kathy had told them about me camping in the wildlife area this summer as they had lots of questions to ask me.

This was a special day in Cable, as the local actors put on a play at the high school. They will be joined by the Cable clowns that entertain between acts of the play.

After a great meal of fried chicken, at least as good as Moms, we all headed to the high school to take in the play and the clowns. The play was called, *'The Girl of the Limberlost'*. It took place in the deep south and was about this young girl that lived in a run down house with her mother in this big swamp called the Limberlost. She was able to catch rare butterflies and sell them for large amounts of money. The performers did a very good job of keeping me interested and I could tell that Savannah really liked the play too. The clowns were full of fun and came out in the audience and really made the people laugh.

The play ended and the people spent a fair amount of time visiting with each other. Savannah and I left and walked to her grandparents house. We held hands and stopped in a dark shadow and kissed. WOW!! That girl is really something. We really had a wonderful day together even if her parents, and later her grandparents, were with us.

I slept on the floor in the living room. The next morning I woke up before anyone was stirring and I lay there thinking about this nice elderly couple that were now both retired but were still very active. They were very happy and seemed interested in many things. Their home certainly was not fancy but it was very nice, well cared for and very comfortable. What a wonderful life they have now but I imagine their earlier years were very full as they raised a family and provided a fine, loving home for themselves and their family. I admired what they have here now and I could see they were proud of their life's accomplishments.

After a breakfast of pancakes, we all piled in Elon's car and headed to the latest development in the Cable area. It was a ski hill called *Telemark*. It was southeast of Cable a few miles and was started by a World War II veteran from Hayward. We could see where the ski runs were down this small mountain called Mount Telemark. Some buildings were being built at the bottom of the ski runs and poles were being placed for the tow ropes to pull skiers to the top of the mountain. All in all, it seemed quite exciting. Elon's Dad said, "They hope to be open this winter. Maybe you all could come up and ski over Christmas." That would be lots of fun assuming we could learn to ski. Those slopes looked pretty steep to me. We drove to Drummond to see where Elon's dad had worked. We saw huge stacks of lumber, a lot of steam coming from the lumber driers and a great amount of activity. Elon's dad had worked with a man by the name of Benson whose son was a terrific basketball player and played for River Falls State College. They played in national tournaments at Kansas City, but never won a national championship. His dad was sure proud of him. The boys name was Neumann.

We returned to the nice house by the Namekagon River. We sat by the river and visited until close to lunch time. I asked if I could take a shower. Man, that felt great.

Savannah and her grandmother made some ham sandwiches which along with potato salad was lunch. We said goodbye, got in the car and headed toward Beaver Brook.

On the way home, we went through the City of Hayward. A man by the name of Spray had recently caught a new world record musky, about 66 or 67 pounds. This giant fish was caught southeast of Hayward in the Chippewa

Flowage. Hayward was having some kind of celebration in honor of the big musky.

Savannah and I got in the back seat on the way home. We held hands and we could not keep from looking at each other. This girl was beautiful!! She sure made me forget about catching trout and nearly anything else. I am only 15 years old and I cannot understand how just being around Savannah can cause me to lose track of time, and act like a klutz. And in general, I get a nice warm feeling about being near Savannah. If she looks at me and smiles, I am done. I really don't know much about girls but I do know that I really like Savannah.

Elon dropped me off at the bridge on Beaver Brook. I thanked the Casey's for a great time at the fair and meeting Elon's mom and dad. Savannah sneaked a quick kiss to me just before Elon stopped by the bridge. We said goodbye until tomorrow noon and I headed for my camp.

I decided to practice my 'Crazy-Legs' Hirsch football moves on the way to camp. Plant left foot, cut right. Plant right foot, cut left around a tree or bush. Look for the best path through the trees and brush. Run hard, cut hard, use a stiff arm, shift the ball (chunk of wood) to the opposite hand away from tackler. I hope to do about one hour each day until football starts. Good night.

**July 25, 1948 - Late.**

We had the picnic at Little Dove and Walking Bear's place. Great food. A big table was set up outside and food put on it. Various chairs were rounded up. Earl and

Margaret are very friendly and took some ribbing from the rest of us. I bet they will get married. Earl is going to enroll at Stevens Point State College and hopes to become a game warden. Margaret teaches near Stevens Point so that sounds like something that will work. Earl has applied for G. I. Bill funds to pay for his schooling. He really seems happy and appears to be getting along just fine. He asked if his friend, Gordon, from Superior came to visit. I told him that he had and he wanted to do a story but I told him no. I said Gordon seems like a great guy and I am looking forward to reading his stories in the *Superior Evening Telegram*.

I asked Mom if my buddies were around now. She said she had seen both of them and she had seen one of the mothers in the store and she asked about you. She fibbed and told her you were not home yet. I asked Mom to tell the boys that I was camping in the Beaver Brook Wildlife Area and to invite them to come to the camp on Thursday, by mid-morning. Tell them to plan on spending the night. Also tell them how to find the trail to the campsite.

We had just started to eat when a strange vehicle drove past. The boys I met at the beaver pond were with this rig. Little Dove flagged them down and invited them to join us for some lunch. They must have liked what they saw so they shut off the rig and helped themselves. I asked Dick, "What is that rig?" He said, "It is called a bug - a poor mans tractor." It had truck tires on the rear, but no box on the back. There was a bed above the wheels and no doors. Dick said, "My dad and older brother built it. It has two transmissions so it can go very slow, if needed. It has a strange looking hitch on the back." Dick continued, "We go into the woods with it to get firewood and logs. It is nearly out of gas so we are on our way to Oscar's Store to get gas. We hope we don't run out before we get there."

Walking Bear went into the shack and brought out a quart jar that was filled with gasoline. He said, "Take this and use it if you run out. You can drop it off on the way back." Little Dove asked, "Is the family finished picking green beans? I have not seen them go by lately." Joe said, "The picking is finished and nobody here is sad about that. Picking beans is a real crummy job."

My folks and Savannah's folks really seemed to like each other. They seemed to have quite a few interests in common. Maybe it is Savannah and me.

Dick and Joe returned with the bug and returned the jar of gasoline. The bug was of great interest to the men and we all went and looked at it. Joe said, "There are others around and one farmer actually plows with his bug." During World War II, tractors were not being made so old truck bodies were modified to work like a tractor.

By late afternoon, the food was all eaten and the cokes and cream soda were gone. Earl said, "Nick, you and I have seen the view of the big woods from the big hill and it is spectacular. Should we see if anyone wants to see it too? If they do, maybe we could ask the owners if we could see the view from their farm." Right now everyone said they wanted to see the view. I asked Dad if he would drive me up to that farm on the hilltop and we could ask if this group could impose on him and his family for a few minutes so the others could see this wonderful view. Dad agreed and the two of us drove to the hilltop and out to the farm. We went to the door and knocked and a kindly, middle age man came to the door. I explained. "I have been camping down in the wildlife area and we were having a picnic and several of the people wanted to view the woods from your hill. Would it be alright if about eight other folks came into your yard so they could view this big woods like you do every day?" The man said, "Of course, they can. Go get them and let them see it."

Dad and I went back and reported the good news. We all loaded into Dad's and Elon's cars and drove to the hilltop farm. Savannah sat on my lap. WOW! We arrived at the farm and got out. The owner came out and said his name was Arthur and we were welcome to go down past the barn and view the woods. There were two young kids peeping out of the windows of the house. It was only about one hundred feet and we could get a wonderful view of my summer home. I pointed out the grove of white pines where the camp was located. Mom said, "It is a breathtaking sight." About that time a passenger train with a steam engine came by on the railroad tracks. What an exciting sight. Steam and smoke coming out of the engine as it moved along at a high speed.

It was easy to see where the bottom of this big valley was and we knew that Beaver Brook ran there. We could see the trestle where the small stream flowed underneath. All in all, it was an exciting view. I was proud that all the people at the picnic could see the woods that was my home this summer. I certainly admired this far away view of the place I had come to love and respect.

The picnic goers broke up and headed for home, as it was early evening by now. Savannah wanted to know if she could meet me at the bridge on Wednesday about noon. That was four days from now. I said I would be there as this might be our last meeting this summer. This was a busy day. To think that all these people came together because of my camping in the wildlife area. I can feel a strong sense of caring, maybe it is love between all of us. Today gave me a warm, good feeling. I really do have good friends at this time. I wonder what the future holds for the people at the picnic. All I know is that right now we are good friends. This was a special day. Good night.

**July 26, 1948 - Early.**

After breakfast I saw a chubby brown critter run into a burrow south of the pine grove. I watched the burrow and after several minutes, the critter stuck its head out. I wracked my brain and finally figured out that it was a woodchuck. This was the first one of these animals I had ever seen. In school I had learned that they are rodents so they have gnawing teeth like beavers, squirrels, chipmunks, rabbits and many more animals. Today I am going to do my Crazy-Legs drills as I go to the house on the dirt road and try to see Dick. Maybe we could spend some time together. He seems like a real nice kid.

I got to the house on the dirt road and walked down to it. No one was outside so I knocked on the door and a little girl came to the door. I asked if Dick was there and the little girl left and soon Dick came to the door. He welcomed me and said, "Come on in and meet my family." We went into the house and there was a bunch of people in the living room. Dick introduced me to all of them, including his mom and dad. All in all, there were seven kids and the mother and father. They all seemed very nice.

Dick and I went outside. We played catch with a baseball for awhile and then Dick showed me another bug that his family was making. It was just about ready. Dick showed me around and then we sat under a tree and talked. Dick said the family was going to move to a house about two miles away, going south across the stream and the railroad tracks and then west across Highway 53. It would be the first place on the right. His family will rent the house. They decided that the winters were very hard as the road got drifted in with snow and it took several days to get plowed out. The family had to do a great deal of shoveling to be able to get to town or school. The decision was made to find another home. Dick said, "We love it here, but it is time to move."

**July 27, 1948 - Early.**

Today I am going to walk past Dick's new home.

**July 27, 1948 - Late.**

I walked the tracks to the dirt road and walked past Little Dove and Walking Bear's home. I crossed Highway 53 and came to the first place on the right. It was a farm and by now I figured out that the cows I saw in the pasture by the swamp and small stream must come here to be milked. I walked past this place to the next road and could see a big farm just up the road to the south. Boy, the crops sure looked good. I turned around and walked past the farm again. Now there was a boy about my age in the front yard. He waved at me and said hello. I waved back and also said hello. We walked toward each other and we talked. His name was Jerry and they were getting ready to move to a new house just on top of the hill by the big farm we could see to the southwest. Jerry seemed like a nice, friendly boy. I told him, "I have seen you with your mom and dad going to work on the fence by the railroad tracks." He asked, "Where do you live?" I told him Spooner. "Wow," he said, "That is strange. We are several miles from Spooner. How did you get there?" "I am camping in the wildlife area by the stream." I said. "Are you camping all summer?" he asked. "Yes, since the first part of June." I replied. "Are you still camping there?" he asked. "Yes, but I will be going home in about a week. Have you been to the beaver pond and the sluice dam?" I asked. Jerry said, "Yes, I have been there about three or four times."

"Last fall when I was in 7$^{th}$ grade, my friend Pete and I discovered both of those places in early October. That was an exciting day as neither of us had crossed the railroad tracks and ventured into that huge woods until that day. It was scary, but exciting." Jerry continued, "Pete and I have been to the beaver pond two or three times this summer. In fact, we were just crossing the beaver dam when we saw someone standing out in the pond fighting a big fish. We watched for several minutes. And just as the guy was going to net the fish, the fish made a huge splash and got away. We ducked back into the brush on the north side of the beaver dam and watched. The guy watched for a while and then turned and walked out of the pond and went off in a southwest direction." "That was me!" I said. Jerry said, "That must have been a big fish." "It was," I replied. "It was a trout of at least four pounds and is very likely still in the beaver pond." Jerry asked, "Is your camp anywhere near the pond?" I said, "Yes, about a few hundred yards to the southwest, on the west side of the stream and in a grove of large white pines. Why don't you come and visit me if you can." Jerry said, "We are going to move soon so I am pretty busy. Let me ask my mom and maybe I could go back with you today."

Jerry was gone for a few minutes and finally came back and said, "Mom said I could go with you as long as I got home by four o'clock so I can help my dad when he gets home." Jerry also said, "When I was in the house Pete called and wondered if we could get together today and go to the beaver pond. I told him about you and asked if he wanted to go visit your camp. He said sure and should be here in a few minutes."

Pete arrived and we met each other. Both Pete and Jerry go to school in Shell Lake and will both be in eighth grade this fall. Both boys are good sized and nearly as large as I am. We headed up between the two barns and over the hill toward the northeast. We crossed Highway 53 and were in Jerry's pasture. The cows have been sold and have been gone for about a week. We followed the trail to the large marsh where the small stream starts. I told of hearing a sound like someone pumping water with a hand pump. I said, "My dad and I investigated and saw the shy poke sitting on her nest with her beak up in the air. Jerry said, "Pete and I heard the same sound, took off our shoes and saw the shy poke also. I wonder if she is still around."

We came to the place where the trail crosses the small stream and Jerry said, "Pete and I belonged to a cub scout pack with three or four other boys when we were in 5<sup>th</sup> or

6$^{th}$ grade. One day we took a field trip down here without our den mother. Someone got the bright idea of throwing a big rock in the water and splashing the rest of us. That started it. We hunted up rocks and had two teams, one team on each side of the stream and we spent at least an hour trying to splash mud and water on the other team. The rocks were big enough so in order to bomb someone, you had to be pretty close to the water so the other guy watches and when you move up, so does he and both deliver their rocks. Then they high tail it out of there before the mud and water hits you. It was fun and we all ended up wet and muddy." It sounded like these guys knew how to have fun.

We crossed the field and crawled through the fence and got on the railroad tracks and walked to the trestle. I said, "Let's go down and follow the small stream. It goes through a real cool place." We followed the stream and both Pete and Jerry looked in pools as we came to them. "What are you looking for?" I asked. Jerry said, "Last fall, after deer season, we were exploring this stream and we saw fish in some of the pools. We had our .22 rifles so we decided to try to shoot one and see what it was. We were surprised to find that we did not have to actually hit the fish to stun it. We picked up four of them and discovered that they were trout. Probably brook trout. We each took two trout home and we both got talked to by our parents for shooting into the water and getting these beautiful trout out of season. And they were pretty sure it was illegal to shoot trout. There was talk about calling the game warden, but in the end, we ate the trout and did not do that again. It turns out that the trout were coming into the small stream to spawn."

We headed to my camp and I pointed out the fox den where the three fox pups lived. We got to camp and they were impressed! I explained how I got food and things from my dad as he drove the train by. Telling how I boiled water and ate trout every other day sounded like a cool idea. Neither of these guys had ever fished trout but were both interested in learning. I told them about all the different animals and birds I had seen. The saw-whet owl seemed to really fascinate both of them. Finding the wolf tracks by the stream got their attention, too. I told about finding Joe Pachoes winter quarters, the trappers cabin and the remains of the logging camp. They both had met Dick and Joe and were looking forward to being friends with Dick.

By now it was late enough that Jerry and Pete had to head for home. They walked up the trail to the railroad tracks. I enjoyed meeting both of these boys and maybe I will see them again. They both seemed to envy my being able to camp all summer. Good night.

## July 28, 1948 - Early.

A pileated woodpecker flew into the pine grove. It began banging away at a dead spot on a basswood growing near the pines. That bird really made the chips fly. In a few minutes, it made a hole big enough for it to disappear into. It continued to make the chips fly out of that hole. Finally, it stuck its head out and it had a big fat white grub in its beak. In a flash, the bird swallowed the grub and disappeared into the hole again. I watched it show itself with grubs in its beak two more times. After about forty-five minutes, it let out a powerful song, not very pretty, and away it flew. What a magnificent sight!

Pileated Woodpecker

**July 29, 1948 - Early.**

Savannah is going to be at the bridge by about noon today.
I sure do miss her.

**July 29, 1948 - Late.**

I got to the bridge before noon. I can hear a car coming.
It was Savannah - driving the car - by herself! WOW!
She pulled up by me with a huge grin on her face. Her
parents let her drive, by herself. She was scared but
excited to be able to make this trip by herself. Her dad
had been helping her to learn to drive.

She parked the car in a space fishermen have parked in

just south of the bridge. We hugged and kissed and about then it began to rain. We got into the car as it rained harder and harder. Savannah had made some sandwiches and she brought two bottles of Coke. We ate lunch and talked. We both realized that our magical summer is nearly at an end. We talked about the things we had done during the summer.

We finally discussed what would happen once Savannah goes back to Antigo and I return to Spooner. We both were going to be freshmen in good sized high schools. Both of us are worried about how that will go. We both intend to get involved in athletics and other school activities. We tried to come up with a date when we could see each other again. Finally, it looked like Thanksgiving would be the first time we could see each other. Neither of us have a drivers license so to drive to visit each other will not work. We also thought Christmas vacation would be another possible time. We promised to write letters, frequently, and make a few telephone calls.

By the time we had discussed our concerns about being separated, we seemed to have worked ourselves into a feeling of excitement toward each other. We hugged and kissed and snuggled in the front seat of Savannah's car. We got more and more excited with each other. We were quite passionate with each other for over an hour. Both of us felt that we wanted to do more than snuggle, but we also were scared and really did not know much about what might follow. We certainly had strong feelings for each other and we had a wonderful afternoon but nothing other than snuggling happened.

Finally, Savannah said she needed to get the car back as

her folks needed to use it. The rain had finally stopped but we must have gotten two inches from noon to about three o'clock. The windows of the car were fogged up but Savannah backed out onto the road and took me up to where the road came very close to the railroad tracks. I figured I would not get as wet walking the tracks to the trail to camp as I would be following the stream. We kissed good-bye and I watched Savannah drive away. I had a very sad feeling. Maybe I was feeling sorry for myself for not being able to be with Savannah until Thanksgiving. This was an emotional day for me.

I had just started walking north on the railroad tracks when I heard a trains whistle just to my south. After the first whistle, the engineer put out several blasts like it was an extra warning. All at once, I heard what sounded like an engine hitting a car. NO! That could be Savannah!!!!! I looked back and I could see a wrecked car on the east side of the tracks by the crossing. My heart dropped. Could that be Savannah's car?

I ran along the tracks and beside the now stopped freight train with a single diesel engine. The engineer and fireman followed me as we ran toward the wrecked car. I was nearly out of breath when I got close to the wreck. There was Savannah! She was standing by another woman and two small children.

As I ran up to her I could see her car setting on the road - not wrecked. Savannah was trying to comfort the woman and the two kids. I gave Savannah a hug and told her how scared I was that it was her car that had been hit.

By now the brakeman, engineer and fireman arrived and

were relieved to see everyone was alright. The car was really munched.

Savannah told me that this car had driven out of the driveway just before the crossing. The car stalled on the tracks but the woman and the two children got out and away from the car. The engineer put the brakes on but could not stop in time.

After the train crew determined that no one had been hurt, they said that they would proceed to Spooner and call the sheriff to take care of the paper work. They inquired if the lady and children could get a ride from someone. The lady looked at Savannah and asked if she could give them a ride home which was about three miles west on this road. Savannah said that she could.

The train finally got moving. Everybody but me climbed into Savannah's car. I could tell that Savannah was nervous and I asked if she wanted me to ride along while she took these folks home. At first she said she could do it but the look in her eyes told me that I should ride along, so I climbed in too.

As we rode towards the families home, one of the kids, about four years old said, "Boy, that was close." We dropped the family off and Savannah turned around and headed back toward the tracks. I could tell she was relieved to get the family safely home. When we came to Highway 53, I told Savannah to let me off there and I would walk through the pasture and get to the track and then to camp. I did not want Savannah to have to go near the wrecked car - besides the sheriff may be there now. I told her how terrible I felt when I thought her car was hit.

We kissed and Savannah drove away again. I really felt sad.

**July 30, 1948 - Early.**

My Spooner buddies, Jim and Jed, should come to camp today. I hope they can make it.

**July 30, 1948 - Late**

Jim and Jed got to camp by mid-morning. They were impressed! I had to apologize for my deception and both boys said they understood. Also, they understood that I didn't want other kids finding my camp and upsetting my plans.

I told them about all the animals and birds I have seen. We looked for the saw-whet owls but could not see them. We went to the sluice dam and then to Joe Pachoes winter quarters. We went back to camp to get fishing gear as both boys wanted to try to catch some trout. I let Jim use my fly rod and Jed used the spinning rod with the French spinner on it. Both boys decided to take off their shoes and wade in the stream as they fished.

We went a little to the south from camp and entered the water there. Jim would fish downstream into the big sweep hole. Jed would fish upstream towards the straight hole. Jim hooked a nice trout and landed it. It was an eleven inch brookie. Jed needed a few casts to get the hang of how to cast with the spinning rod. All at once, I heard a big splash and I could tell Jed had a fish on the line. I was able to net it for him and it was a twelve and one-half inch brown trout. Both boys continued fishing, getting farther apart.

I stayed with Jim and he eventually finished working the big sweep hole and moved downstream to the upstream sluice hole. He was using worms for bait and soon caught a nice eight and one-half inch brookie. Just a little further into the hole he caught an eleven inch brown trout. I told Jim he could catch only one more trout and I went upstream to see how Jed was doing. He was just getting to the northeast curve hole. As I approached, Jed got a hard hit and hooked a nice trout. I got to him in time to net the fish, a twelve inch brookie. I told Jed only one more fish. He moved further upstream and made a nice cast, right near the bank with an undercut and after a short retrieve he got a very hard hit and the trout jumped out of the water and the spinner came out and flew right at Jed. He ducked but was impressed with that trout that got away. He made another cast and caught an eight inch brookie.

We headed back to camp but I continued downstream to where Jim was fishing. He had not caught the last fish yet but, all at once, he got a bite. I got to him and netted the trout. It was a fat ten inch brookie. That was enough trout for supper so we headed for camp. We cleaned the trout and I got a fire going so we could boil some water and fry the trout.

After supper we just sat around and talked. Jim told of spending most of the summer living with his grandparents in Milwaukee. He really didn't like the big city, but there were some interesting things to do like going to the zoo. He did play on a summer baseball team and enjoyed that. Jed told of his trip to the west with his grandmother.

Mount Rushmore, Glacier National Park and Yellowstone National Park were places they visited and he was really impressed by all he saw. When they got back to Rochester, Minnesota, he and a neighbor boy spent the rest of the summer painting his grandmothers house along with her garage. I rearranged things in the tent so all of us could sleep in there. We talked about lots of things, including Earl Burke coming into camp. I told about the time Earl had a breakdown and thought he was being attacked. I did not tell them about Savannah. I might tell them about Margaret, but I don't know yet. We are going to the beaver pond tomorrow and also to the trappers cabin. We also will follow the trail to Dick and Joe's house. By then, Jim and Jed plan to head for home.

**July 31, 1948 - Late.**

After breakfast, we crossed the stream at the sluice dam and went to the beaver dam on the pond. Jim and Jed had never seen a beaver dam and were very impressed with this dam which was about four and one-half to five feet high but only about sixty feet wide. We walked around the pond and came to a spot where the beaver had been logging. Both boys were very impressed by how the beaver could gnaw a tree down and cut off the limbs and drag it into the water. We could see a beaver lodge on the northeast part of the pond. Aspen was their favorite tree and as we looked around, we saw most of the aspen that was left were a fairly long distance from the pond and the dam. Maybe the beaver will have to leave to find a good supply of aspen. They also may eat the bark off other trees although it doesn't look like it here.

We left the pond and went to the trappers cabin under the

blown down tree. I told them about finding his diary and that he eventually left the cabin and took a job on the railroad. He was killed by a train hitting the hand car he was riding on during a big snowstorm. We headed south until we came to the trail that led to Dick and Joe's house. Jim and Jed were wondering if we would ever get there, but we did. Dick and Joe were not home. They were helping some cousins put up hay. Jim and Jed really liked the old cars sitting around and they were impressed with the bug that was being built. We hiked back down the trail, crossed the stream at the sluice dam and got to camp. I rounded up some sandwiches made with Spam. I needed two cans and it took a full loaf of bread. We sat around camp for awhile and then Jim and Jed headed up the trail toward the railroad tracks.

I could tell that they enjoyed the visit and deep down wished they could have camped also. I said, "Maybe next year." After the boys left, I picked up my chunk of wood that I pretend is a football and did my Crazy-Legs Hirsch practice, running in the trees and underbrush, planting my foot so I can cut to avoid tacklers. I did that for about an hour and I was really tired.

Since today is Friday and Dad will be coming past with the train, I put a few things in the bag that I won't need in camp anymore and get up to the tracks. Because Mom and Dad are coming Sunday to visit me and help break camp, anything I can give to Dad is that much less to carry to the car.

**August 1, 1948 - Early.**

Last day before I break camp tomorrow. I decide to run to

the reservoir and try to catch a northern pike. I don't know if they will bite on the French spinners I have but I am going to try. If I catch any, I will give them to Little Dove and Walking Bear. Once I got to the railroad tracks, I ran as fast as I could, stepping on every other tie. I took the road nearest the marsh to get to the reservoir and started casting with my spinner. I had to avoid certain places because of weeds and stumps.

On about the fifth cast, I got a strike. It pulled the reel handle out of my hand and I could tell it was a nice fish. I could not hold this fish and it pulled out line against the drag. It ran about seventy-five feet and then stopped. I kept pressure on it and it began to move. I took up line and was able to move this fish toward me. It took another run of about forty feet. I could move the fish again to a point about twenty-five feet in front of me, but for at least ten minutes it just laid there. Finally, it began to move and took out line again but only about twenty feet this time. After another twenty minutes or so, I finally could see this big fish. It took another ten minutes to finally get the net under it or at least most of it got in the net. This northern pike was thirty-six inches long and I estimated it must weigh twelve to fifteen pounds. It took me close to an hour to land it with my light spinning tackle. It was a beautiful fish.

I had a short piece of small rope that I carefully threaded through one of the gills and out its mouth filled with long sharp teeth. Now I could carry it and I headed for Little Dove and Walking Bear's place. When I got near their shack, Little Dove came running to meet me. I told her it was for her and Walking Bear. She was excited about the fish and then she gave me a big hug. She was happy about that fish and possibly seeing me too.  She has always been very friendly - almost like an aunt or maybe a sister.  Since I don't have a sister, I really don't know how one might act.  Anyway, I do like Little Dove, not like I like Savannah though.  I told her I was going to break camp starting tomorrow and by Tuesday I will be back home on High Street in Spooner.

The Washburn County Fair is starting on Wednesday and football starts in a little over a week.  I need to get in shape so I don't get munched!  I told Little Dove that I probably would not see her again until next summer sometime.  She said she will really miss me and yes, they will go to Alabama for the winter.  They are planning to return again next summer.

She thanked me for the fish and then gave me another big hug and this time she kissed me.  When I went to leave she grabbed my right hand and held it for several seconds.  I finally pulled away and started walking towards the railroad tracks.  Little Dove walked with me for about a hundred feet and then she said good-bye.  I could see tears in her eyes and after about five seconds she whistled at me and when I turned around, she blew a kiss to me.  I know my face was red but I turned and started running toward the tracks.  That lady sure seems to like me.  I ran the tracks to my trail and I was pretty tired by the time I finished running.  I decided to do fifty deep knee bends before I headed for camp.

Since Mom and Dad are coming tomorrow, I probably won't fish any more.  In thinking about my fishing experiences this summer, I concluded that I had amazing luck catching several large trout, at least for Beaver

Brook, which is not a very large stream and its all recorded in this diary as well as in my memory. Catching that big northern today was an exciting experience. Good night.

## August 2, 1948 - Early.

I had just finished breakfast when I heard something walking fast. It was west of me and I stood up to see if I could see it. It was a wildcat, or bobcat! It was about forty feet away and headed north. It seemed like a good sized cat, maybe 25-30 pounds. It continued to the north without seeing me but it must have caught my scent because it stopped and smelled the air and looked all around. Finally, it saw me and the hair on its back and neck bristled as it looked at me for about five seconds and then it bounded away. What a beautiful animal. Mom and Dad are coming today.

## August 2, 1948 - Late.

Mom brought her great fried chicken, fresh bread and a few cookies. We talked about Jim and Jed visiting camp. Also that I had met Dick and Joe and the next day I met Jerry and Pete and they came back to camp with me. They seemed like nice friendly boys. Both are one year younger than me. I told about catching the big northern and giving it to Little Dove. Mom asked if Little Dove appreciated the fish. I said she did. From the way Mom asked that question, I wondered if she knows something about Little Dove that I don't know. Anyway, I dropped the subject.

Dad and I decided what should go home with them today. Most of the extra clothes and blankets can go today. Dad is going to take tomorrow off from work so we can finish breaking camp and take everything home with us. By late afternoon, we had three packs prepared to carry to the car. The fish poles, net, creel and hip boots were part of my load. We went up the trail and got on the railroad tracks and headed for the car. Mom was having a harder time but she made it. It was a good thing the car was not any farther away. Good night.

## August 3, 1948 - Early.

Last day in camp! I am sad. This past two months of living in this camp have been exciting and wonderful. Meeting the people that I did, especially Savannah has been a great experience for a young, mostly naïve, fourteen, now fifteen year old boy. I think I have grown up a great deal in two months. I must be about the luckiest boy in the world to be able to camp and fish in this amazing wildlife area. It is truly a gem and the best part is that it is owned by all of us and we all can use it. There is beauty here that anyone could appreciate. I am amazed at all the different animals and birds I have seen while camping. My favorites are the three fox pups and the five saw-whet owls.

I have really come to admire the trout that live in this stream. They live in a stream that can flood or nearly dry up. Somehow these very colorful, hard fighting trout manage to find things to eat and are very, very wary. I had exceptional luck being able to catch as many large trout as I did.

I plan to take the tarp down, strike the tent, fill in the slit trench and restore the fire ring to the way it was before we made camp here. I plan to leave this campsite with no trash left and except for places that we walked, the entire area should look like it did before we arrived.

## August 3, 1948 - Late.

I carried everything up the trail and left it in the woods beside the trail. Dad came walking down the tracks about midmorning. We needed two trips to the car but finally we got the last of the camp loaded in the car.

After the car was loaded, Dad gave me a hug and said he was proud of me. That is not like my dad, but it meant a lot to me. Both Mom and Dad have been very supportive of this venture. I am sure they have had plenty of reservations about the entire affair as it is possible for bad things to happen, such as accidents, sickness or people doing harmful things.

We started for Spooner and High Street. Except for a few minutes in Spooner when I dropped Margaret off, and when we passed through on the way to the Tri-State Fair, this is the first time I have been in Spooner since early June, about two months ago. I didn't see any big changes as we drove toward home. We arrived home and Mom came out and gave me a big hug. She also said she was proud of me and was glad I was home. I will have to say that I am proud of myself too. I thanked both Mom and Dad for letting me have this wonderful summer. It was a great experience and meeting Savannah was the highlight of my summer.

This is the last entry in this diary, 'The Boy and the Brook'.

# Epilog

Nick and Savannah were faithful about writing letters and calling each other on the telephone. They met during vacation times whenever possible. After graduating from high school, they both enrolled at Stevens Point State College. During their second year in college they were married, but they continued working toward degrees in biology. After graduation, Nick got a job teaching science and Savannah began a long career as a trout fishing writer, author and lecturer. She eventually wrote four books on trout fishing and over fifty articles for outdoor magazines. She was in constant demand to speak at various conventions. She continued as a representative for the Mepps fishing lures from her home town of Antigo, Wisconsin.

Nick got a science teaching job at Drummond, Wisconsin and Nick and Savannah were able to buy her grandparents home on the banks of the Namekagon River at Cable, Wisconsin. Both Savannah and Nick were guides and had many successful fishing excursions, mainly on the Brule River. They had two children, a daughter Mackenzie and a son, Ronald.

Elon and Kathy retired and live at Antigo. They still own the cottage near Birchwood, Wisconsin.

Nick's parents are retired and live in the same house on High Street in Spooner.

Earl and Margaret got married and are now retired. They live in Margaret's home on the lake near Birchwood. Earl became a game warden and Margaret taught school for thirty-five years.

Little Dove and Walking Bear came back to the cranberry marsh for three more summers, but then stayed in Alabama.

Dick and Joe both live in Minnesota but both own property very near their parents home on the dirt road near the Beaver Brook Wildlife Area.

Jerry moved to Oregon and has only visited once or twice.

Pete lives east of Spooner and visits the wildlife area often.

Even though this story is fiction, it is based on facts and tries to reflect the way things were in 1948. I hope you have enjoyed this story.